DRAGONS WITHIN

Embracing Her Fire

Other Books in the

Dragons Within

Anthology Series

Dragons Within: Claiming Her Wings

Dragons Within: Guarding Her Own

DRAGONS WITHIN
Embracing Her Fire

BALANCE OF SEVEN

Dallas

Dragons Within
Embracing Her Fire

Copyright © 2021 by Balance of Seven
All rights reserved. Printed in the United States.

All stories are copyrighted to their respective authors and used here with their permission.

No part of this book may be used or reproduced in any manner whatsoever without written permission except in the case of brief quotations embodied in critical articles and reviews.

The stories in this anthology are works of fiction. Unless otherwise indicated, all names, characters, businesses, places, events, and incidents in this book are either the product of the authors' imaginations or used in a fictitious manner. Any resemblance to actual persons, living or dead, or actual events is purely coincidental.

For information, contact:
Balance of Seven, www.balanceofseven.com
Publisher: dyfreeman@balanceofseven.com
Managing Editor: tntinker@balanceofseven.com

Cover Design by Eben Schumacher Art, ebenschumacherart.artstation.com

Developmental Editing by Leo Otherland, roseoftheotherlands@gmail.com

Copyediting and Formatting by TNT Editing, www.theodorentinker.com/TNTEditing

Proofreading by Amanda Mills Woodlee

Publisher's Cataloging-in-Publication Data

Title: Dragons within : embracing her fire / Balance of Seven.
Description: Dallas, TX : Balance of Seven, 2021. | Series: Dragons within; book 3. | Contents: The Burning Bones / Nikolai Wisekal – Brazen / C. D. Lombardi – Balancing the Scales / Chaz Beebe – A Dark and Terrible Beauty / K. A. Moore – A Dragon's Hoard / JoAnne Turner – The Web Speaks / D.B. Smyth – Queen of the Underworld / Rachael Denessen – The Gift / Jaumarro "Joy" Cuffee – That Which Binds Us / Lex Night – Legend of Ardmire Castle / Sianyn Leigh – All Stop / L. C. Jenkins – Conversion / Ynes Malakova. | Summary: The strong women in these twelve stories claim their dragon-like traits for their own good and the good of those around them.
Identifiers: LCCN 2021948435 | ISBN 9781947012097 (pbk.) | ISBN 9781947012103 (ebook)
Subjects: LCSH: Character – Fiction. | Dragons – Fiction. | Women in literature. | Fantasy fiction. | Short stories. | BISAC: FICTION / Fantasy / Action & Adventure. | FICTION / Fantasy / Dragons & Mythical Creatures. | FICTION / Women.
Classification: LCC PS509.F3 D73E 2019 (print) | PS509.F3 (ebook) | DDC 813 D73E--dc23
LC record available at https://lccn.loc.gov/ 2021948435

25 24 23 22 21   1 2 3 4 5

To those whose dragon within is shunned by society:

May she give you the strength and courage

to accept her and take pride in her

in the face of opposition.

Contents

Introduction

For many of us, 2020 was a year of uncertainty and indecision. So many things changed so quickly, it felt like *normal* would never come back, and we looked to 2021 with hope for better things. Yet for me, 2021 has proven to be a year of labor and hardship.

In the early months of the new year, I was accepted into a small short-run magazine. The other contributors and I were invited to share our work and get to know each other. I did so, though with the warning that I wrote dark, gritty things and readers should take care, and I went about the business of contributing to the magazine. Over a month later, I was unexpectedly let go from the project because one of my fellow contributors had read a piece of my work and was "concerned." Without even a chance to defend myself or to explain what had prompted the writing of the piece in question, I was simply told to leave. I took this ejection hard because, for all my conscious life, I had wanted nothing more than to write words that could help people, the way books had given me life and purpose in my darkest times. I wanted to leave hope for the hopeless in the form of paper and ink, but if, instead, what I was writing was hurting people, then what was I doing? Should I even *be* writing?

After a few conversations with dear friends, I moved forward and continued writing—only to meet with a similar situation a few months later. I had joined a group of enthusiastic writers who were inspiring me to write with passion. Once again, I shared my work and warned my fellow writers that my writing wasn't for everyone. Yet despite my warning, I was again dismissed from the group. I found myself hurt, lost, and yet again wondering what business I had creating words if those words were doing more harm than good.

I ached, but I kept moving on. Some short time after this second expulsion, I began conversing with a reader who had commented on my work. Over the course of our conversations, I confided in my newfound friend about my concerns regarding whether I should be writing. And this person—whom I had never met in person but whom I connected with on so many levels of understanding—responded that not everyone found hope in rainbows and unicorns. That for some, hope like that, in stories filled with light and softness, didn't feel real. Or was unattainable. For some, hope was found in stories of darkness and broken characters who, despite everything, kept moving on.

What my friend said affected me deeply. I held onto their words and pondered them, and I started to wonder if perhaps whether I should be writing was the wrong question. Instead, I began to ask myself, "For whom do I write?" The answer I found was that I did not write for those who already had hope or who lived in the light. I wrote for those in the shadows, who looked for a light they could relate to. With that realization, I embraced my fire as a writer, as well as the understanding of exactly how much responsibility my power carried. I had the ability to harm as much as help, and I needed to use my fire with care.

As you, dear readers, enter this book full of tales of women embracing their fire in the face of circumstances and societies that tell them they should not, I invite you to embrace your own fire. To know your power is to know all the responsibilities that come with it, yet this knowledge is worth understanding. Enter the worlds of *Dragons Within* and dare to find a piece of yourself there.

Leo Otherland

The Burning Bones

Nikolai Wisekal

Uzim couldn't remember the last time she had felt human, but her aching bones enjoyed reminding her that she was. Every morning, she heard their creaky whispers:

Don't go out in the sun.

Sleep a little longer.

She grunted and groaned through the lies. She'd never missed a sunrise, and this day would be no different. As she passed through the night's last shadows, her bare feet stepped onto ruby glass. It was still cold from the night before, and for a moment, the chill was the only sensation she wanted to feel. Slowly, golden light pulled back the curtain of night to reveal shimmering black dots among red as far as the eye could see: the black bones of dragons resting on the ruby-red sands of the Fireglass Desert.

Watching the first rays pass over her dark skin, Uzim again wondered why dragons came to the desert to die. She'd lived there for forty years and knew the name of every dragon, but she still had no answer. Scratching her bald head, she smiled, reminding herself answers were often less pleasant than questions. Turning back to the skeleton looming behind her, she cracked her knuckles and prepared for the day's work.

She stripped down to her wrinkles. The first time Uzim had done this, her clothes had not survived. Since then, she'd done the work nude. The scandal this would have caused back at court still made her smile. From what little she'd heard, the few who remembered her called her many things: madwoman, heretic, and traitor were some of the kinder ones.

She called herself a bone reader. Each morning, as the sun rose, the bones remembered. The air inside the dragons' bones grew warmer, and the memories of their fires were stoked until crimson veins grew across the black skeleton. The bones called to her with a thrumming pulse, but she stared at the skull, following the rivers of veins to the base of the spine.

"Let us see who you are."

She laid tender fingertips where spine met skull. The black bone was smooth as marble and hot as fire, and she sucked in air at the familiar pain. In the same breath, the name of the dragon roared into her mind.

She inclined her head from the force of the memory, while her every survival instinct screamed for her to show deference, pulling her to her knees. The throb and ache of her joints were but a whisper in her head compared to the knowledge ahead, so she stood, hands still on the bones, and began tracing the veins. More roaring memories came with every step.

"I was born in summer," boomed the dragon's baritone memory. *"A child of mountains that pierced the sky."*

Uzim witnessed its lineage and waited to hear more.

"There I hunted the beasts of the mountain. The winds carried me from peak to peak."

Uzim smiled at the first memory of tasting blood and the surge of flight. Gray peaks beneath her, endless blue above! She blinked out cool tears. In forty years, she'd flown hundreds of times, but through their eyes, the first time never lost its magic.

She paused when the smooth skull ended, becoming long, razor-sharp teeth. Here she hoped for the best. The first kill was a goat he had ambushed. He pinned it beneath his claws and bit through its vertebrae. Sweet blood rushed over his teeth as bones crunched, and it was over.

More hunts and kills flowed into Uzim's head as she traced the teeth. By the last tooth, not a single man, woman, or child had died in his maw.

With practiced hands, she finished the skull and, without breaking from the memories, continued to the body. Time passed, and the inevitable fate of all dragons came closer. Uzim didn't bother trying to stop the tears as she witnessed the slow decline from a lord of the sky to thinning wings and failing sight. Meanwhile, his fire ate him from the inside, and his final breath consumed every muscle and scale into ashen oblivion. As she reached the tail, Uzim crumpled, her mind and sight deep in that funereal inferno, until her sight faded into darkness.

When Uzim woke, she expected to be freezing in the middle of a desert night. Instead, soft furs against her body kept the cold at bay.

"Welcome back!" Akestis called.

Uzim pushed away the blanket. "I never left."

A sharp whistle echoed through the skeletal shelter. "A rump worthy of royalty."

"And you are only worthy of the ass that carries your goods," Uzim shot back, stepping deeper into the shadows to slip into her desert clothing.

"Perhaps, but a man must appreciate all beauty lest he never lay eyes on it again."

The sound of pouring liquid reached Uzim, and she turned to eye the young merchant. He was smiling without reserve and scanning the shadows fruitlessly. Uzim stepped forward from where he wasn't looking and took the tea he offered, sitting beneath the light of the moon to enjoy the company of one of her few living friends.

"What are you trading this time?"

"Some spices and metals, both of which have been in high demand since the blockade began."

Uzim stopped drinking. "Blockade?"

Akestis's smile shrank. "Bad blood between your old home and Aksul across your desert," he offered, then sipped his tea.

Uzim felt faint human memories respond to the name: long hours spent with her teachers, princes she had been promised to wed.

"Baako isn't a soldier or war hungry. Why would he do this?"

"He wouldn't, but . . ." He sipped his drink, never looking at her.

"But?" Uzim pressed, setting aside her tea.

Akestis stared into his cup. "Baako was overthrown."

Uzim couldn't breathe but forced herself to speak. "Ekene was a soldier, but he was loyal. He wouldn't—"

"Baako and Ekene are dead," Akestis blurted out, looking at Uzim out of the corner of his eye.

Two of her brothers, dead in one sentence. That left just the one. "Is Udo safe?"

Akestis reached for a bottle, and when he popped the cork, something sweet and sharp filled the air. The merchant sucked it down like a man dying of thirst.

"Udo led the coup," he finally whispered.

"Proof?" she whispered back.

Akestis swallowed from the bottle like he would never taste it again. Then he reached into a pouch and laid two rings in Uzim's hands. They were carved with her brothers' names, gifts from their parents. Bits of the brass shone in the moonlight, but some parts were stained. She caught the scent. The stains were dried and flaking, but they gave off the copper stink of blood all the same.

Fury, both her own and from the dragon memories, rushed through her like fire to tinder. So many words and questions wanted to rip their way up her throat. Uzim leaped to her feet, age forgotten, stepped past the dragon's ribs, and screamed.

Every drop of air she had came out in a sound that clawed the air until it became a roar from the dragon memories. The air just beyond her teeth grew bright with fire, like a sun in the night.

The dragon sheltering them, and all those before him, offered her more fire, but memories of Baako's kind wit and Ekene's offers to spar brought tears streaming down Uzim's face. Akestis was no longer smiling, only holding out the bottle.

Uzim drank greedily, but the numbing warmth never came, just the distant sense of burning down her throat. She still drank; if she breathed fire again, she wouldn't stop. Once she'd swallowed the last drops, her grip tightened until cracks spiderwebbed across the bottle.

"He sent you?" she asked.

"At the end of a spear."

"Any message?"

"Meet me at the edge of the desert and our home. We'll talk at the first dragon grave you found."

Indignant rage from the dragon memories matched her own, until the bottle shattered in her hands.

"Thank you for the message."

As she brushed away shards of glass, not a single drop of her blood spilled.

"Best be on my way. Goods won't sell themselves." Akestis's flirting smile was back from force of habit. Uzim turned to him, and his smile shrank as his eyes widened. "I'm just the messenger. I had no hand in their deaths!"

"Defile nothing, and you may cross the desert in peace," Uzim declared, her voice layered with a dragon's basso.

She reached for her staff, the only bone the dragons had allowed her to take. It was the same obsidian black that sucked in the moonlight and curved to a wicked point. She nodded at Akestis and set off toward the home she'd long ago abandoned. To Jarza.

Low winds whipped the sand against Uzim's skin. The abrasive sensation never stopped, and she didn't care. Step by step, she marched toward her first dragon grave, guided by her memory and the dragon's remains. She stopped only when her gut refused to be ignored.

In the shelter of a dragon grave, she chewed dried lizard meat until it was a wet pulp, before tearing off another bite. Thinking of all the questions she wanted to ask her brother brought back other memories. Udo had cried when he crushed a beetle by accident. He couldn't stand to strike his sparring partners. He had always tried to make peace between Baako and Ekene.

Looking at the ruby glass beneath the bones, Uzim saw crow's-feet surrounding her eyes. Amazing changes could come in one day; she had no way of knowing what forty years had done to her little brother.

Between the angry chewing and the questions, the day got older, and the sun sank into the horizon. She grabbed her staff, bowed to the bones in thanks, and set off again.

Her first clue she was close was the stench of steel and sweat. It didn't tell her how many miles remained, but it did tell her she was expected. She followed the smells through another night, more than once staring down venomous snakes who dared bare their fangs. One she speared on the end of her bone staff. At least she'd have something fresher to eat on the way back.

Her next clue was the noise. Put enough men eager for a fight in one place, and between the shouting, scraping of armor, and clashing of swords, they created the worst music in the world: the melody of war.

Hours later, she could even see the white-and-green tents of the army. She refused to eat or drink, eyes fixed on her destination. Closer still, she realized they'd encamped around the dragon grave!

Udo had a lot to answer for.

The sky was half dark by the time she approached the first patrol. Uzim sent them back; as convenient as horses or even camels were, she preferred to keep her feet on the ground. Closer to the camp, the sentries stood straight as iron rods as she passed. None of them made eye contact. So it was wherever she went: silence and averted gazes.

Udo's tent was pitched to drape over the dragon's snout. Uzim remembered the dragon's name, and its memories followed. This dragon had traveled the world to learn! She'd seen the sky dance with colors at night. She'd been called upon by nomad tribes and empires to trade for her knowledge.

All of that was one thought away for Uzim, and Udo was using the dragon's skull as a prop! Uzim walked faster. Answers were owed.

Guards surrounding the tent stood at the ready. The last rays of sunset glinted off drawn swords and lowered spears, while arrows rested against bows. All the tension made Uzim's skin itch, but she remembered Akestis once saying a joke could break tension.

"If you all step aside, you can shit your armor in peace," she said.

A rare daytime breeze passed, and for a moment, that was the only sound. None of them laughed, but a great many smiled. The ones at the tent flaps stood aside.

Uzim passed through the emerald tent flaps and stepped into a palace. Every bit of ruby glass was covered by carpets. She sank two inches just standing still. The naked torsos of servants ran among silk-wrapped privilege. When she inhaled, the air was a mix of fruit perfumes and sweat. She didn't recognize any of the men and women, but the sound of it—the scent of it—echoed her childhood. Formal affairs of lies and excess. Tiresome was what Uzim had called it as a child, and decades later, the description still fit.

Then she heard the clash of steel.

Like gilded moths to a flame, the men and women gathered toward the sound. Uzim skirted the edge of the crowd, trying to spy the throne by the dragon's teeth. It was empty except for the hammer and chisel her father had used to carve his laws and proclamations.

"Come on!" shouted a familiar voice. "If you're not trying to kill me, what is the point of your sword?" The mocking tone was new.

"My king, I—"

A whistle of air interrupted the second voice, and again came the clash of steel.

Uzim put her staff to work smacking ankles and threw in elbows when the crowd didn't part fast enough. There were glares and outrage, but they all moved aside. The screech and hiss of steel was coming faster now.

By design or by accident, just as Uzim came to the inner circle, Udo stepped forward and buried his scimitar in his opponent's gut. Her little brother turned her way. The boy she had known was now a bearded man with gold-fastened braids hugging his skull. A warrior's style but gilded. Uzim might have laughed at the idea of a gilded warrior, but the dying man was already turning the golden carpet red.

Bloody gold is honest gold.

It was a saying coined by some long-dead sadistic poet king. Inspired by his own words, he'd charged the royal weavers to make a carpet from gold thread, and then he'd watched his subjects bleed it red. Udo had apparently taken up the tradition.

Just as Uzim was about to say something, her brother picked up his opponent's sword.

"Beautiful!" He held it up, and torchlight reflected off ripples of folded steel and a golden hilt. His silk-wrapped advisors cooed their appreciation. Then he turned to the kneeling, bleeding man.

"Seems you were more showman than swordsman. Always thought you were a bit gutless!" Udo laughed, and like an echo of mockingbirds, the advisors laughed along.

Uzim stepped forward. Udo stopped laughing, and the entire tent quieted.

"Ah, my dearest sister, Uzim. People of Jarza, rejoice. Your princess has returned! Truly, this is a joyous day!" The mockingbirds raised their hands to clap, but Uzim's patience for theater was at an end.

"End his suffering, as the tradition dictates!" Her voice carried the hint of a dragon's growl.

Udo's eyes narrowed, but in one fluid movement, the scimitar sliced off the man's head.

"Cut away a piece of the carpet, wrap his head in it, and send it to his widow," Udo commanded. Servants rushed forward to obey, and he faced Uzim without blinking. "As is tradition."

As the gruesome work was done, the advisors shuffled in place, more than a few eyeing the nearest flap.

"Matters of state need tending. Leave us!" Udo shouted. The patterned-silk mockingbirds flew away, practically trampling each other.

"Would you join me for a meal?" Udo asked.

"I don't have much of an appetite," Uzim lied.

Udo shrugged and began stacking a plate. "I was beginning to wonder if Akestis would actually find you."

"You made him fear for his life," Uzim shot back.

Udo turned, raised an eyebrow, and looked her up and down. "It was effective."

Uzim reached into her pocket and produced their brothers' rings. "Explain this!" She didn't feel anything draconic in her voice, but the guards outside shuffled.

Udo took a bite from his plate. "Family heirlooms should go to family."

Uzim wanted to claw the smirk off his face. "How can you call them family? You murdered them!" This time, she growled in contempt.

"They were murdering our country!" Udo shouted back.

Uzim didn't have a response. Taking advantage, Udo walked over to the throne and lounged in it.

"Baako and Ekene were disbanding the military and giving away hard-won lands. They were giving our enemies a chance to invade in vengeance." He bit meat off a bone. "I tried reasoning with them, but they only spoke of the trust it would create, of how peace was the way forward. War gave us our nation. It broke the borders between warring tribes and made an empire. Peace has only ever given our enemies time to plot. I couldn't just stand by—"

"You condemn them," Uzim interrupted. "Yet all I hear is that they were trying to save lives and spread peace."

Udo's placid expression grew tight with a smile that showed too many teeth. "Soldiers give their lives to the nation. Glory in victory is the debt we owe them, not disbandment so they can build roads and farm. We have workers and farmers aplenty. We need more lands for our people to thrive. No matter how many times I explained this, they wouldn't listen. So I taught them their final lesson."

Uzim's fingers curled around her brothers' rings. "Why kill them? Why not exile? Why not send them to me?"

"I offered, but they did not share your madness in choosing this." He gestured at the skull. "When you left, it was a price our family and nation paid." He pointed a cleaned bone at her. "Settle your debt to the people, Sister, and make Jarza great again!"

"Save the speeches for your fools and speak plainly."

"I've killed for lesser insults, Sister."

Uzim closed her eyes and let the dragon memories flow. When she opened her eyes, her sight was vibrant, the shadows illuminated in pale silver. She stared at Udo, who dropped his plate.

"Try."

"The Aksul blockade is not working," he answered quickly. "Some of our allies are sending aid to our enemy. To end this, we need you to guide us along the shortest route through the Fireglass Desert."

Uzim smiled with a mixture of human and dragon teeth. "To what end, Brother?"

"Don't be dense, Sister. You are in an army camp."

At that moment, her memory of him was the only reason this arrogant bastard king still drew breath.

"Jarza is great enough," Uzim said, her voice deepened with a dragon's rumble. "Take your ego and steel away, Brother. They are not welcome." She turned away.

"We will cross without you!" Udo shouted.

"You will wander and die of thirst."

"Seize her!" he shouted. Armor scraped and steel hissed as every guard from outside the tent stepped inside.

"Stand aside, and you will live," Uzim promised.

"Ready to be as bloody as me, Sister?" Udo asked.

Uzim stared at each of the guards, whose weapons gently trembled. "In defense of my life, yes."

A scraping sound came from behind Uzim, and she turned back to see Udo standing on his throne, hammer raised and chisel pressed against one of the dragon's fangs. Ice ran through Uzim's veins for the first time in decades.

"Udo, you can't—"

"Can't I?" he sneered and swung the hammer against the end of the chisel. The strike of metal against the bones rang through the air, while the dragon memories in Uzim's head screamed in pain. She clung to her staff for support.

"Not even a crack yet!" Udo proclaimed. "Maybe we can mine

these for armor and weapons!" He slammed the hammer against the chisel again.

Through teary eyes, Uzim saw the tooth begin to bend away from the jaw. Another slam, another ringing tone, and another scream brought Uzim to her knees.

"At last, you kneel for your king." Udo sounded closer, but his words were distant echoes to Uzim. Every ounce of her focus was spent on keeping the screaming dragon memories from flooding over her own.

"You will apologize, you will guide us through the desert, and"—something cold and flat pushed under Uzim's chin, forcing her eyes up to Udo's sneering face—"you will obey your king!"

Uzim found it in herself to spit in his face, and every last dragon memory chuckled. Udo wiped the saliva away and, in a too-calm voice, said, "The hardest lessons must be taught consistently."

The hammer's head left her chin. When she looked up, Udo was charging toward the skull.

"No!"

Udo didn't answer. Instead, he swung the hammer like a sword and, with a warrior's ululation, broke the fang away from the dragon's skull.

The dragon memories fractured. Where Uzim used to know things, now she only thought she knew, or maybe she never remembered.

"Take her away and call in the smiths," Udo commanded. "Let's see what they can make out of this."

Cold, sharp points rested at Uzim's throat and spine, but Udo's words cut deeper and worse. She tried to make the pieces of the dragon memories come together, but they slipped apart along fracture lines. Even as she tried, the magic of the broken dragon bone lost its shape and sought something familiar.

Slowly, like the first sparks from flint striking steel, burning rage gathered. Uzim's dragon eyes could see the crimson veins in the bones begin to drift into the air. When she breathed, brimstone smoke filled her nose.

In a moment of clarity, Uzim remembered the day this dragon had first felt pain. The crimson veins answered with a roar of anguish only she could hear. They writhed away from the bones, reforming into a twisted mockery of their former shape. The veins moaned at the misery that was becoming their identity. The sound ripped tears from Uzim's eyes. Udo and all the guards were blind to what was happening as the veins rushed out of the tent. Winds began to whistle and rise in answer to the roar.

"Udo, you have to—"

Something wooden smacked the side of Uzim's head. The world spun while her head throbbed, inside and out.

"I must do nothing. I am—"

Udo stopped short as the winds of the storm began carrying red sand through every opening in the tent.

"Shut the flaps!" Udo shouted.

The stench of brimstone was stronger now. The memory of the dragon was fading as fast as the crimson veins had from the bones.

"Is this—"

Udo's words were cut short by the sound of tearing fabric. Voices rose as a carpet flared into a small fire. Servants and guards doused it.

"What is it?" Udo demanded.

One of the guards was shoved forward. His eyes were wide as he approached, but they flinched closed as he held up the carpet for all to see. Smooth patterns at the edges led to a crater of charred fibers flecked with red glass. At the center was a sizzling red mass. To Uzim's eyes, it could have been a badly shaped arrowhead.

Udo turned, pointing his hammer at Uzim. "What have you done?"

Uzim didn't answer, just looked up and waited. The screeching storm winds grew silent, replaced by human screams.

"What is going on?" Udo shouted.

One guard opened a tent flap and fell back, face aflame. The others skittered back, but the tent ceiling tore again and again beneath falling shards, each spreading fire. Udo shouted orders, which were ignored as everyone fled.

Uzim recovered her staff and stumbled toward him. "Stay with me if you want to live."

Udo glared but followed Uzim into the dragon skull. From between the teeth, they watched the army burn.

All through the storm, Uzim willed the heat and flames away, giving them the smallest possible shelter. All night, the storm raged. Uzim closed her eyes against the sight of the fire-glass rain breaking against men and women. Only the hiss of cooking flesh interrupted the screams. Udo clutched his knees and muttered, but Uzim could not hear his words above the bubbling of the red sands. They waited as the memory of dragon fire turned the desert sands molten. Even by the next evening, if she had relented her will for a moment, Udo would have been ash. Through the screams and after, he never shed a single tear. He only stared.

When the sky cleared, Uzim used her staff to break open their red cocoon. Willing the heat elsewhere, she stepped free, and Udo followed. Outside, a preserved horror greeted them. Uzim's stomach turned, and Udo fell to his knees.

Everything was entombed in red glass.

"Why?" Udo whimpered.

"Before the dragons came, these were known as the Ruby Wastes." Her words didn't seem to reach Udo, but he looked up when she tapped him with her staff. "Did you never wonder why they called it the Fireglass Desert?"

He looked past her at the frozen soldiers. Bones and flesh alike were lit by the sun shining through the glass. Beyond them huddled men and women. In some places, they clung to each other so tightly, it seemed the glass had fused their bodies together.

"Why?" Udo asked again.

"Your pride was the cause of this, not me."

Udo shook his head. "Why did you let me live?"

Uzim flicked his temple, and he flinched. "Because it is my last mercy to you. Now follow!"

Uzim willed the heated glass to cool as they walked. Looking back, she saw Udo's eyes were watching her heels. She kept her eyes up, taking in the permanent rictus of everyone in camp.

At the edge of camp, she tossed a waterskin to Udo. "That should keep you alive long enough to reach Jarza."

Udo's shock finally broke, and he jabbed a finger at Uzim. "You've left your people without soldiers to protect them!"

"The desert is enough of a barrier against most. Those who try your foolishness will meet the same fate." She pointed beyond Udo, but he didn't turn. "Go tell our people what their king has lost. Perhaps you will see the value in peace when you have no other choice."

Udo's mouth opened, but he said nothing. Instead, he started to walk back home.

"Farewell, Brother," Uzim whispered and started off back into her desert.

brazen

C. D. Lombardi

A gentle breeze blew through the whispering reeds of Dawn Lake Meadow. It continued across the lake, rippling the surface as it pushed through the fire-red hair of the young woman standing on the bank.

Here it comes.

The sun crested, and rays of ruby light, the color of her eyes, cascaded across Dawn Lake, rolling across the surface like lava from a volcano. *So beautiful.* Brazen let herself enjoy the sight for a few moments, until the sun had risen enough for the effect to diminish.

Okay. Time to practice. But first . . .

Brazen looked across the lake and surveyed the meadow surrounding it, making sure no one was watching. Next, she closed her eyes and took a deep breath. The meadow was encircled by a small forest, from which drifted the scents of a rabbit, a squirrel, and possibly a deer. The latter was too far away for her to be certain.

All clear so far.

Last, she opened her tall, pointed ears and listened intently. Only the rabbit—now two—and the squirrel were within earshot.

She opened her eyes and smiled. Shaking away tension, she held out one hand and focused. A spark appeared on her palm and sprouted into a small flame. Her eyes widened, and the flame grew larger, splitting into two, then four. She held out her arm, and the flames danced along it.

Little red lights of joy.

She gathered them together into one large flame and started turning it. Faster and faster, until it became a small whirlwind of fire.

I have never understood why Shicela will not let me try new things. Why am I not allowed to let the flame loose? Grandma always says I should be mindful of the darkness that runs in our family, but it is nothing I cannot control, and practice makes me better. Brazen smiled. *Plus, it feels so good to let them out to dance and twirl.*

As she got lost in thought, Brazen's concentration faltered. For a moment, the fire turned dark, tentacles of black flame peeking out from the inner core.

"Brazen."

That sounded like her mentor, Shicela. The "Ice Queen," though Brazen would not dare call her so to her face. The coldhearted leader of the ice dragons hated the nickname.

And if she caught Brazen out here practicing, there would be trouble.

Brazen looked toward the forest on the other side of the lake. No one was visible yet. She relaxed and glanced back down, just in time to see the fire devil leap from her hand toward the meadow floor. Instinctively, she threw it into the lake.

A massive steam cloud rose where it hit. *That is worse! They will know.* Focusing her fire, she heated the surface of the lake, forming a low cloud above it. *Maybe I can pass this off as early-morning fog.*

Shicela exited the forest, accompanied by Lanosa—a red dragonette, like Brazen, and her best friend. They spotted her and circled the lake.

Surveying the lake as they approached, Shicela raised an eyebrow. "That fog rolled in fast, did it not?"

Brazen flushed. "No, it has been like that since I got here. In fact, it was denser earlier. It appears to be dissipating now that the sun has risen."

Shicela squinted and shook her head, her white hair dropping snowflakes across her body. "I need to keep a closer eye on you. Two, even."

Shicela was close enough now for Brazen to feel cold. Brazen shivered. She was not sure if it was from Shicela's cold attitude or presence.

Lanosa hugged Brazen. "I am glad we found you. They are calling for everyone to gather in the amphitheater."

Brazen sighed. "Is it mandatory?"

"Yes," replied Shicela. "We must attend."

The amphitheater was huge. The lower levels were reserved for the wurms, those who had already become full dragons. The upper levels were for the dragonettes, the young humanoids. Each level in between, larger than the one above, represented further growth. Despite its large size, the amphitheater's curve amplified sound so everyone could hear every level.

Lanosa and Brazen went to the very top, while Shicela settled one level down.

After a few minutes, everyone settled in, and the great doors on the ground level opened. Two elder wurms escorted a human woman dressed in battered chain mail into the main circle. Gasps echoed through the amphitheater.

Silvertoung of the Golden Scaled royal family, the oldest great wurm and leader of the dragon community, emerged from a set of doors on the opposite side, flanked by an escort. As he stopped in front of the human, the rest of the Council of Wurms took their appropriate places, forming a semicircle.

Silvertoung addressed the human. "It has been many years since your kind has walked here. I understand you used an ancient rite of calling to request all members be present. I must admit, that was brave of you. Few have the authority. Can you prove you have the right to use it?"

The nubile human shook short blonde hair out of her eyes and stepped forward. "My name is Avanol Hammier. Headen Hammier was my great-grandfather, five generations removed. Grandfather was friends with the dragon council back then. According to writings, you, Silvertoung, vowed that if we ever needed, we could call upon you."

Buzzing whispers and shock shot through the community.

"Yes, Avanol. Your claim is true. We will listen to your plea but listen only. Afterward, we shall decide what to do. Please continue."

Avanol straightened and stood as tall as she could. "I come from the land to the west, Grecalan. We are a peaceful people: farmers and artisans with families. We are no threat to anyone. Recently, a new overlord, Malic, proclaimed himself ruler of the land. He and his army take whatever he wants and have levied impossible taxes. Punished are those who do not pay, and sometimes their lands are taken. They end up working for him. I, and a few hundred others, fought back."

She bowed her head, pausing for a moment. "Most of us are dead. We will fight to regain our land, but we do not have the means or strength. Many of us have had our homes ransacked, lands stolen, or worse. I come before you today asking for help, for us and for the other villages. I call for justice. Will you please help?"

Avanol stepped back and waited.

Silvertoung scratched his beard, his long claw rasping through the hair. "We will deliberate and discuss. Please eat, drink, and rest. We will return shortly."

Silvertoung and the rest of the council left the now-quiet amphitheater. The doors closed with a loud, echoing thud. Then everyone started talking at once.

Brazen grabbed Lanosa's hand. Her eyes sparkled. "I wonder how they will help. Maybe they will send a fleet of elders or greats. It sounds so adventurous."

Lanosa cast her eyes down, her cheeks turning red. "I do not know what they will decide."

Several minutes later, the doors reopened, and Silvertoung and the council reemerged.

Brazen smiled. "That was fast."

"Avanol, descendant of Headen Hammier, we must decline your request."

Avanol's eyes widened, and her mouth gaped. "I have traveled a long way to see a debt repaid, and you decline?"

"It was not just my decision. That debt was incurred a long time ago. Both our worlds have changed since then. In the past, we have tried helping others, only to be betrayed or used. The younger races are not honorable. They would use our aid for personal gain. We now prefer to keep to ourselves and not get involved with others."

"Is that a definitive answer? Do you speak for everyone here? Will no one aid us in our time of need?"

Silvertoung reared up, irritated. "Avanol, I give you my word. If anyone wishes to aid you, I will not stop them, but no one will volunteer."

"Is there no one who will help us? Please?" Avanol's shoulders slumped. She looked older, aging ten years in just a few moments.

"I will help. I will help them get their lands back."

The voice cut through the amphitheater, clear to all tiers. All heads turned toward the top level. Brightening, Avanol scanned for the dragon who would aid her and her people. When she saw young Brazen standing near the top, she sighed.

The elder Fircalla stood on her hind legs and flared her red wings. "Brazen, these are adult matters."

"Grandmother, I turned one hundred last spring. By our laws, I am an adult."

"Bah, no! I forbid it. You are way too young." Fircalla folded her wings and turned away.

Silvertoung closed his eyes. "No, Fircalla. I gave my word that if someone offered to help, we would not stand in their way. As an adult, Brazen may make her own choices. Brazen, understand you will be on your own. We will not get involved."

Brazen swallowed but smiled. "I understand." Turning to Lanosa, she whispered, "Come with me."

Lanosa shook her head. "I do not know what you are thinking, but no. I am sorry. Good luck, Brazen." She got up and left.

Silvertoung paused, verifying no one else wanted to speak. "This session is done. I wish you the best, Avanol and Brazen." He turned and walked out, the council close behind.

Brazen spent one last morning at Dawn Lake Meadow, watching the daily greeting of the sun and trying to memorize every detail. She sighed. She would not see her favorite place for a while.

Afterward, she met with Avanol at the stables, where the human had prepared the horses and gathered provisions.

"Thank you for volunteering to help us."

"I am glad to help. I also need to leave and find out who I am. I cannot do that under the scrutiny of my teachers."

Avanol reached into her saddlebags and pulled out a long blade, bigger than a dagger but not quite a sword. A small red stone was embedded in the pommel. "We have a tradition among my people. When we welcome a comrade-in-arms to our cause, we give them a small token of appreciation." She handed the blade to Brazen. "Unguarded is thy back. I give you this blade, and offer mine as well, to protect you through the trials ahead."

Brazen's heart warmed, and she blushed. She had never received such a gift. "Thank you. I will guard you as well."

Avanol smiled. "Not quite the ritual response, but it will do." She stuck her hand out. Brazen, unaccustomed to the ritual, placed her hand out as well. Avanol laughed and grabbed Brazen's hand in hers. She then drew her in and hugged her. Brazen smiled and hugged her back.

Fircalla arrived to see them off. "Is this what you truly want?"

Brazen placed her saddlebags on her horse. "Grandmother, I am tired of being sequestered. All I do is restrain myself. I am never allowed to let the fire loose. This is a grand opportunity for me to be my true self and help these people."

Fircalla bowed her head. "Brazen, be careful. We reds are among the most dangerous. Our fire can spread quickly and do more damage than others. Remember your teachings. Avanol, I will leave you with an ancient saying among dragons: Only ask for oxen if you have tried and like oxen. Many think they need oxen, but what they desire is cow."

Avanol shrugged. "What does that mean?"

"Be careful what you ask for. You may get it, even if it is not what you truly need or want."

Avanol's brow furrowed, and she tilted her head to the side. "Thank you?"

They left the dragon city atop the mountains and worked their way down a winding path. Many rocks and landslides hid the path, and several times they had to detour. When they made it to the base of the mountain range, a sea of sand and rock stretched before them to the horizon. They turned southwest and headed across the barren plain.

They rode in silence, each lost in her own thoughts.

A few hours later, Avanol turned to Brazen. "I must admit, I had expected more or at least someone older. Please do not take offense. I appreciate you volunteering to help, but how much difference can one dragonette make?"

Brazen smiled. "Allow me to demonstrate." She dismounted, glanced around out of habit, and walked a safe distance away. They were still in an open dry area, almost a desert. She held out her hand and produced a flame. She fed the flame, allowing it to grow. Twirling her fingers, she twisted it into a cyclone.

I do not have to hold back anymore.

Excited, she fueled the flame with more energy than ever before. It became a roaring tornado, fire spewing forth in all directions.

Avanol backed away, the light reflecting in her eyes. She smiled. "This is something we can work with," she shouted over the roar of the fiery tornado.

Brazen stopped feeding the fire and pushed it away, but the tornado had other ideas as darkness surged up her throat.

Down. Easy. Breathe. You can control it. Just relax.

The steadying thoughts helped calm her, and she regained control. The fire roamed about for a few more minutes until it finally gave out.

Avanol was still smiling when Brazen turned back to her. "Impressive."

They traveled for two more days before meeting up with Avanol's companions. They were few, only six in all. Each wore armor of a different caliber, many pieces of which were so damaged, they were falling apart. They had never seen a dragonette, or any kind of dragon, before, and they treated her like a mystical sorceress. None besides Avanol would meet Brazen's eyes. They seemed afraid yet relieved she had joined them.

The first village they wished to reclaim was not far away. As they approached, four soldiers came to attention, unsheathing their weapons.

Avanol began to speak, but Brazen cut her off. "Do you mind if I try?" Avanol relaxed, letting Brazen take the lead.

"Hello," Brazen called to the soldiers. "We have come to liberate this village. We do not mean anyone harm. We ask that you gather your people and leave this village in peace."

The closest soldier looked at Brazen and the rest of their group. Then he laughed and turned to his fellow soldiers, who joined in. "Did someone put you up to this? If so, they are not your friend. Drop your weapons and coins, and we may spare you."

Brazen dismounted, whispering to Avanol, "Have everyone back up a suitable distance."

As Avanol waved the others back, the soldier grew angry. "Where do you think you are going? Are you listening? Do you want us to make an example of you?"

One of the other soldiers fired a warning arrow.

That was all Brazen needed to justify herself. Heat rolled off her, and her red hair flew up, forming a fiery mane around her face. She blasted fire at the archer, who screamed as his armor and body melted.

The closest soldier's eyes grew wide and fearful before he turned and ran. The rest followed.

Brazen turned to Avanol. "Have someone ensure they all leave the village. I will deal with any problems."

They followed the same routine for the next several villages. They met very little resistance once Brazen demonstrated her power. There were eight villages and towns between the dragon city and Malic's keep.

Grateful, each village provided whatever mounts, armor, weapons, and provisions they could. Some townspeople even wanted to help and joined their band. Soon, they had a small gathering of twelve.

When they arrived at the sixth village, four soldiers waited for them, carrying no weapons and showing no signs of resistance. Once they were within earshot, their leader spoke.

"You are not helping these people. Sure, you can run us foot soldiers off; we cannot defeat you. But once word reaches Lord Malic, he will send an army to stop you. You will not be able to fight off an entire army of hundreds or even thousands. Once you are dead, who will stop him from taking back every town? They will pay the price once you are gone."

"He makes a good point," called a man standing a respectful distance behind the soldiers. He was tall and muscular, with a scarred face and metal-studded leather armor. From his belt hung a sheathed dagger and broadsword. Other villagers came closer to listen as the soldiers walked away.

"My name is Evidar, and I have the same question. Once you leave—dead or by choice—who is going to protect these people? Your actions will have consequences that cannot be foreseen. I am a veteran mercenary, and I could not hold back an entire army, even if they could afford me."

"We are taking the fight to Malic," Avanol insisted. "He will not be around to come back and harm anyone."

"You are committed to taking him out, then? Do you need any help? I would be willing, but my help would cost a portion of the loot we find."

"We would welcome the aid."

Evidar scoffed but then smiled broadly.

The next town held a delightful surprise. Instead of soldiers, several townsfolk stood at the town's edge, waiting for them.

In the center of the crowd stood a tall, middle-aged man. He might once have been strong and strapping, but now he bore only a portly midriff. His body was wrapped in cloths of many colors, including a white one with *Chief* spelled out in black lettering. As their group approached, the chief turned to a small child standing next to him. From a pillow the child held, he picked up a multicolored headdress bearing three large plumes of red, blue, and yellow. He put on the headdress, sucked in his gut, and stuck out his chest.

"He reminds me of a peacock," Brazen whispered to Avanol.

The chief spread his arms wide. "I am Chief Artamaya. Welcome to Ratachi." He beckoned them closer. "We heard of your liberation movement that you plan to take to Malic himself. To show our gratitude and eagerness to take part, we chased the guards away from our own city."

"Yeah, right," Brazen overheard from someone in the crowd. "Malic recalled them. Just like the chief to take the credit, though."

Artamaya clapped in delight. A small band played a fanfare, and children threw small, colored fabrics into the air.

"We will hold a feast and dance in your honor," Artamaya announced. "After the feast, we would appreciate a display of your fire."

"Thank you, Chief Artamaya," Avanol said, "but this is really not necessary."

"It is a gift from our people. We even have lodging arranged for you."

"We thank you, but we must turn down the lodging. We will make camp here, just outside your town." Brazen's decision was met with looks of disappointment among her group, and she added, "However, there may be individuals among our group who would appreciate the lodging."

The chief grinned. "Yes. Yes. All are welcome."

Artamaya led those who wanted to stay in town to their homes for the night. The rest made camp, including Evidar, who kept apart from the others. He set up his tent and then started into town alone.

"We have plenty of time before the festivities begin," Avanol called after him.

"I am heading into town to find a decent drink. They have to have at least one tavern in this town."

Once Brazen and Avanol were alone in Brazen's tent, Brazen expressed a concern she had. "He mentioned a dance. I have been told most of my people's dances are not considered proper by human standards."

Avanol sat on a bedroll. "You could dance for me, and I could let you know."

"Thank you. I would like that."

Brazen opened her saddlebags and pulled forth a sheer pink cloth. Taking off her traveling clothes and leaving on only her intimates, she donned the sheer dress. The pink of the cloth perfectly matched the color of her scales. Once dressed, she rolled her hands and arms in a circular S fashion, twitching her hips back and forth and occasionally undulating her torso.

"We try to express our dragonette forms as much as we can; once we undergo the change, we can never move like this again."

Avanol blushed. Her breathing sped as she shifted uncomfortably. "I can see why. You had better stop for now. I do not think that would be appropriate for this dance. Let me teach you a warrior's dance we can do together."

As the time for the festival approached, Brazen and Avanol met up with the rest of their entourage. The banquet was held in an enormous hall filled with three long rows of tables in the shape of a U. The head tables were reserved for Brazen, their group, and the honored citizens of Ratachi.

After the feast, a small band started playing music. Servants pulled the tables to the walls, clearing room for dancing, which several couples took advantage of.

Avanol turned to Brazen. "Care to dance?"

They began by facing each other, bowing, and offering each other an unladen hand. Then they moved around each other to the beat of the music. Once back-to-back, they mimicked drawing swords, though the dance was traditionally performed with actual weapons. They feinted and attacked unseen foes. They twirled and swung, stepping to the beat of the music.

They danced until they faced each other, and Brazen grinned. "Do you trust me?"

"You know I do."

They sheathed their imaginary swords and took each other's hand. Taking the lead, Avanol spun Brazen out and pulled her back in. Upon Brazen's return, six small fires appeared, three on each of her arms. The bright-red, star-shaped fires started dancing to the music. As the dance progressed, it became faster. More fires appeared, dancing in a circle around them.

When the song ended, a faster one began, and Brazen gave in to the music, moving outside the boundaries of the dance. She took the lead and danced around Avanol. Avanol caught her hand and pulled her in close. As their eyes locked, Brazen flushed. Her hair changed to flames as wisps of fire fell from her body. The temperature of the room rose. Brazen sensed the heat was becoming too much and tried to tone down the flame, but caught as she was in the throes of passion, she could no longer hold back.

Instead, she let go.

This fire's freedom was different than Brazen was used to. It was accompanied by emotion: care and consideration for others' safety. Brazen's eyes changed from red to a deep blue, and the fire changed with her. The cores remained red, while the outer flames turned blue, shades of pink and purple cascading in between. Fire enveloped both Brazen and Avanol, forming a tall column of swirling flames. The flame's touch did not feel hot but warm and gentle, like a lover's caress.

As the couple danced, the world around them disappeared: all the people, the tables, everything. Time stopped. They might as well have been the only two who existed.

The flames joined in the middle. Brazen pulled Avanol in close for an embrace, pressing their foreheads together. Two large flames— one red, one blue—erupted from the column. The red transformed into Brazen's form, and the blue took on Avanol's. Then the flames started the ancient dance again.

The song stopped, but they continued to dance. The two flames dodged, weaved, and twirled, bearing swords of flame in place of imagined ones. Arcs of fire trailed the swinging swords. Brazen's internal fire rejoiced in this new feeling of freedom, like a prisoner released back into society after a years-long imprisonment.

Plus now she could share it with Avanol, her closest friend. She never wanted it to end.

Finally, the two flames embraced, became one, and then separated. Sparks fell from where the two touched.

While the fire had no effect on Brazen, she realized it might affect Avanol in ways she did not understand. She sent both flames flying back into the column, ending the dance.

The universe returned as Brazen and Avanol realized the rest of the world existed. People stood back from the dance floor, clapping. Children danced, trying to mimic the pair's movements.

The chief's mouth hung open. "That was incredible."

Brazen's eyes changed back to normal. When she tried to walk, she swayed, and Avanol caught her. "I believe we shall retire for the night."

The chief nodded. "Yes, yes. Get some rest."

Avanol walked Brazen back to her tent, opening the tent so Brazen could enter. "Good night, Brazen."

Before Avanol could leave, Brazen grabbed her tunic and pulled her inside. That night, and all nights thereafter, they shared a tent.

The next morning, Avanol noticed Evidar had not spent the night in his tent. "He did not return from the tavern. He did not attend the banquet last night either. Did you see him, Brazen?"

"I heard him during the night. He was talking with someone whose voice I did not recognize."

"We need to watch him. Evidar is number thirteen, an unlucky number for me."

The land changed as they traveled closer to Malic's keep. The countryside became more fertile and not as flat, providing different levels for the growth of various crops. Folk appeared to be better fed yet more oppressed, their faces sallow and haunted. Many had lost hope. They no longer lived; now they served.

The eighth town, Copla, was the last before Malic's keep. The town was unique, as there was no one in the streets. It was silent, with no visual signs of life. Brazen closed her eyes and listened. People were nearby. She could hear breathing in all directions and a few hushed whispers quieting others.

"Where is everyone?" Brazen surveyed the streets and surrounding areas. "All the homes and businesses are closed? This makes little sense."

She approached an empty market stall and held her hand over the cooking area. "The coals are still warm."

Avanol tried another vendor. "They must have left in a hurry. I can still smell roasted pork. Something is wrong. I feel like we are being watched."

"You can feel the electricity in the air, the tension."

A small brown-haired boy appeared down the street and stared at them. "Where is everyone?" Avanol called.

The little boy pointed at Brazen and then at Avanol. "Are you someone important? You must be special. Your pictures are on the board in the town square."

"Can you show us?" Avanol gestured for the boy to lead them.

They followed the boy to the town's announcement board. "See. There you two are."

Posted on the board were three bulletins. Two contained a picture of either Avanol or Brazen, with the title *Dead or Alive*. Underneath the pictures, a reward of a thousand gold coins was offered for Brazen and five hundred for Avanol. The third bulletin warned people the penalty for aiding them in any way was death.

Avanol shook her head. "News travels fast, but . . . where did they get someone to draw us? The artist did a decent job; the pictures look like us."

A tall, thin woman came around the corner and called to the boy. "Tomas, get over here."

The little boy turned and headed to his mother. He waved goodbye as his mother picked him up and ran out of sight.

Brazen sighed. "I doubt we will get any help here. Though we did not see any soldiers; maybe they left before we got here."

Avanol frowned. "Maybe, but I have a bad feeling—"

Several arrows whistled past her head. Avanol grabbed Brazen and ran to the opposite side of the street, while the rest of the group scattered.

Brazen turned back as one archer came into view. She threw a fiery dart, which hit him in the chest. The archer had no chance to scream before he fell facedown.

"Wait here." Avanol went to examine him. When she returned, shock had settled across her face.

"What is wrong?" Brazen asked.

"That archer was not a soldier." Avanol's voice shook. "He had no uniform, and the bow was very crude."

"You mean—"

"Yes," Avanol interrupted. "He was from Copla. He must have wanted the reward. People are desperate. Gather everyone and leave."

They left Copla quickly. Once on the other side, Malic's keep was only a stone's throw farther. The keep was simple but strong, with a tower at each of the four corners and a gatehouse. The walls were topped with parapets, behind which archers crouched.

The group crested a hill to find an army of five hundred standing on the other side. They were organized in columns and rows before the keep's main entrance.

A pale, elderly rider waved a white flag at the front of the army.

The rider lowered the flag. "I am Felmont, speaker for Lord Malic. My lord wishes to parley."

Avanol raised her eyebrows. "Malic wants to discuss terms of surrender?"

Felmont sneered. "Please do not confuse a discussion of the situation with any kind of surrender. I can guarantee that will not happen as long as we draw breath."

"Then what does Malic wish to discuss?" Brazen inquired.

"*Lord* Malic! He has authorized me to give you and your group the reward of gold coins offered for your capture as compensation for your time. All you have to do is leave without causing further issues."

Brazen's eyes lit up. *I have yet to start my hoard. A thousand gold coins would be a good start. Avanol could take the rest and help others if she wanted.*

Brazen shuddered, clearing her mind. "If I were to accept your offer, would you leave the villages and surrounding towns to their own governing? With little or no taxes?"

"Just how could we pay our soldiers and other expenses? Running a kingdom is expensive. No, that also will not happen."

Atop the battlements, several archers had notched arrows. In the middle stood an older man, taller and broader than the others. He, Brazen realized, was the one in charge, Lord Malic.

Without warning, several arrows came flying toward the group. Though most missed, one ripped through Brazen's shirt, almost drawing blood.

Brazen's face reddened with anger. "Your lord would attack us during parley?"

Felmont's horse was already wheeling back toward the keep. "I think it is safe to assume parley is over." As he rode away, Malic's archers launched more arrows at their group, which was out in the open, with little cover.

Avanol raised a shield and turned to Brazen. "How dare he! Malic planned this from the beginning: get us in archer range and take us out. He will not hurt you. Not while I still breathe."

Brazen's heat rose. She turned to her comrades. "Everyone, retreat as far from me as you can." She paused. The entire group except Avanol had drawn their weapons and were advancing on her.

"You heard him," Evidar spoke to the group. "You saw the posters. Fifteen hundred gold split among the eleven of us is quite a lot. Join us, Avanol. Stand down. We can split the gold twelve ways, or even thirteen if we can convince Brazen to cooperate. She just has to go home. We do not need to fight. I have been in contact with Malic's men. Malic guarantees us safe passage home or wherever we want to go."

Brazen's eyes flared. Flames fell from her hair as it rose into the air. "Avanol was right. You are untrustworthy. That night at the tavern, you met with Malic's lackey, did you not? Leave, while you still can."

"Come now, everyone, she cannot get all of us." Evidar grinned and pulled a long dagger, adding it to the sword he already had out.

The other members unsheathed their own weapons, but they did not appear as confident as Evidar.

"The rest of you feel this way also?" Brazen had had enough. "Avanol, run. Run as fast as you can. I do not want to see you get hurt."

"Please be careful, Brazen."

As the eleven men circled Brazen, more arrows flew. One hit Evidar, bouncing off his armor. Brazen's heat was still rising when several of the men charged. It was too late, though. Their metal weapons grew so hot, they dropped them. Wooden weapons exploded. Men screamed as their armor and clothes started smoldering and blazed. Even the arrows being launched at them disintegrated in midair, their arrowheads falling to the ground as molten slag yards before reaching the group.

Brazen lost control. She threw fire at her comrades, the people she had traveled with. Her fury at being betrayed fed the flames. One by one, they burned. Evidar turned and ran as he burned, but Brazen took him down with a fan of flame sharper than any blade, cutting him in half. The body that fell to the ground was no longer recognizable as human.

Still furious, Brazen turned to the keep, her hair flowing like magma. The ground below her feet melted as she walked toward her new target.

Felmont was attempting to get inside the keep, but the gates were still closed. With Brazen's approach, he turned his mount and started riding along the wall.

Brazen would not allow him to escape. She gathered a gigantic ball of fire and launched it at Felmont. The fire enveloped him, and both he and his horse went down. The rest of the fire exploded against the keep's wall, melting rock, stone, and mortar to leave a gaping hole.

The soldiers in front of the keep lost their composure. Many of them threw down their weapons and yelled their surrender. However, Brazen was too far gone. Within her, the black and vile feeling rose. She could no longer contain it. She screamed and breathed fire for the first time.

It was not ordinary fire but hellfire. Blacker than night, the fire she breathed absorbed the surrounding light, making it hurt to even look at it. She felt like pieces of her soul had turned as black as the fire she exhaled. The dark blaze contained a life of its own. Everything it touched turned to ash and smoke. It traveled of its own free will toward the soldiers, most of whom fled, trying to save their lives.

The hellfire had other plans.

The hellfire danced, taking each soldier as its partner. It tracked and killed all five hundred and then attacked the keep. Brazen watched the beauty of the black fire burn and destroy.

The black fire is even prettier than the red. How can Shicela and Grandma be against something so beautiful? It makes me happy. Yes! My black flames are happy to be out, burning, feeding.

Deep inside, Brazen felt every one of the soldier's souls scream with death's release, and she rejoiced.

She fanned flame once more, this time across the parapets. Those who remained either ran or died.

Except Malic, who still stood atop the wall, his face red with heat. With a scowl, he launched daggers at Brazen, but none came close to hitting her.

Approaching the gates, Brazen flung two raging fire tornadoes at them, and they went down without resistance. The tornadoes continued into the courtyard, followed by Brazen. Hellfire had destroyed the front walls and towers and was making its way to the side walls.

Drawing his sword, Malic jumped down from the crumbling parapets, aiming for Brazen. "If I have to die, at least I will take you with me." They were his last words. He was a trail of soot before he ever reached the ground, and even that soon disintegrated.

A few hundred people cowered in the rear of the courtyard. Brazen was so consumed, she did not care that those who remained were not soldiers but civilians. In that moment, it did not matter. She continued until there was nothing left of the keep. Neither stone nor living creature survived. She leveled everything.

It was only after she had destroyed everything that Brazen realized what she had done and fought to control the flames. She calmed down.

Over time, the flames went out. Many places still burned, but with regular fire.

In the distance, Brazen heard Avanol call, "Are you okay?"

Brazen turned toward her friend and started crying. "No. I am not." Her tears sizzled as they rolled down her face.

Brazen fell to her knees. As she cooled down more, her tears flowed freely. "I should have listened. My teachers, my elders—they told me to take things slow, to learn discipline. Not to let my fire loose. Now I have incinerated all those people, even innocents."

Avanol knelt beside her friend. "Think of everyone you saved and helped in the villages. You liberated the land of Grecalan. Even in Copla, they will thank you once they realize Malic is gone. Stay here and relax. I will look around. There has to be something around here to help Malic's victims."

Avanol had changed. When she spoke, there was a slight shake in her voice. The tremor had never been there before. Avanol's eyes saddened Brazen the most. They were wide and frightened.

Several minutes passed until Avanol returned. She struggled to keep her voice calm. "I . . . I found the gold and more. I will get the horses loaded, and we can get you home. The gold will help us rebuild."

Brazen looked into her friend's eyes. "You know I would never do anything to harm you."

Avanol looked away. "I know." Then she closed her eyes, sighed, and whispered, "I know."

As they returned, they avoided the villages and towns. Still shaken, they avoided all other people.

When they finally reached the dragon city, Avanol said her good-byes to Brazen. "I will not forget you nor everything you have done for us." She left then, heading home to a liberated land with riches to help those in need. It was a new era for her and her country. Fircalla, Shicela, and Lanosa were waiting for Brazen at the entrance. As she approached, Lanosa ran to Brazen and hugged her.

Surprised, Brazen returned the embrace. "How did you know I was back?"

"Shicela saw you from afar."

Fircalla wrapped her wings around both Brazen and Lanosa. "It is good to have you home." Shicela, cold as ever, remained where she was.

Brazen told them of her journey and everything that had happened. She could not hold back the tears and cried once more.

Shicela nodded. "As I have been saying for many years, you need discipline."

Brazen sniffled. "Shicela, you were right. Grandmother too. I still need a lot of training. I have a lot to learn. Shicela, will you help me?"

Shicela smiled, a rare sight. "Of course, little one."

Fircalla retracted her wings and furled them against her back. "I will help as well. The dark fire runs in our family, though I had hoped it would skip you. Untrained, you are a danger to everyone, including yourself."

The next morning, Brazen visited Dawn Lake Meadow. She watched the sun make its glorious arrival, but beautiful as it was, it was not quite the same. Brazen turned away from the lake to find Shicela waiting near the forest. They had a full day of training ahead.

One day, the lake would once again bring her joy.

Today was not that day.

balancing the Scales

Chaz Beebe

beware the roaring onyx sky
Before it blazes red.
Choking smoke will linger
As the foolish all lie dead.”

“That’s just an old song.”

“An old warning,” Daeso corrected as he strummed the last chord. “They say the Elders will eventually get so angry that the dragon will be sent, leaving no one alive.” He strummed as he pretended to think. “I bet the roaring refers to you pitching a fit.”

“But that would never happen to me!” Jeul screamed. “I’m a good girl. A gem! That’s what Mom says.” She stuck her tongue out.

Daeso pursed his lips and tilted his head as he laid the guitar on the couch beside him. “Yeah, yeah.” Daeso pitched his voice higher. “My name is Jeul. My mom named me that because I am such a jewel to have in life. I never do anything wrong just because of my name.” Daeso ended the imitation with his hands clasped together along one side of his head and batting his eyelashes.

Jeul kicked Daeson in the shin. “I am as good as I can be! I try my best not to make mistakes! I don’t want the dragon to come for me!”

Daeso rolled his eyes and stroked the bruise blooming on his shin. “Yeah, you are *totally* the kindest little sister I could ever have.”

Jeul stuck her hands on her hips. "I'm going to tell Mom you're being mean to me."

Staring at Jeul, Daeso bowed deeply, sweeping one arm toward the front door. "After you."

"I will tell Mom! Don't make me do it!"

Without rising from the bow, Daeso continued to stare, pursing his lips and raising an eyebrow.

Jeul stamped one foot. "Fine!" She hurriedly put her shoes on and headed out the door.

Daeso picked up his guitar and began strumming as he slowly followed her. "Thank you, Sis. Just what I wanted." He shut the door behind him, then began playing his guitar and singing as he followed the gravel path to the open-air shops.

The marketplace was full of stands overflowing with baskets of various produce and tables of goods in many colors. Even so, many an eye lingered instead on a certain young woman in a handmade green sweater, which shimmered in the sunlight as she moved.

All morning, villagers had sought Ji out as she wandered among the shops. They came for advice and the gems she provided—gems they believed were magical and could help them with any issue. Her progress through the marketplace was slow, but she didn't mind. She sought atonement through sharing her treasures, and the slow progress was an effect of that choice.

"Thank you, Ji," said one young mother, who clasped Ji's hand and continuously kissed it. "We will never be able to repay you! Without the rainbow moonstone you found for us, the doctor says our boy wouldn't have made it through the night."

The man behind the young mother bowed his head to Ji as he bounced a young child in his arms.

Ji made a full bow in return. "It was my pleasure."

An old woman passing by gave a small smile. "When will you have a family of your own, Ji? I know you've been eyeing a certain someone." Her smile grew wider, and she waggled her brows.

"Oh, Mother Acum!" Ji shook her head, her smile turning embarrassed. "I doubt he even knows I exist."

"I highly doubt that!" With a wink, Mother Acum walked away.

A moment later, Ji heard music that always made her smile. She began walking to the rhythm of the tune, which guided her forward through the crowd. Focused on the music as she was, she was unprepared for a young girl to slam into her legs.

"Oof." Ji struggled not to fall. Once she found her footing, she smiled down at the girl. "Hi, Jeul."

"Ji!" Jeul's face lit with joy, and she raised her arms, jumping up and down. "Save me! He's being mean to me."

Ji picked the girl up and propped her on her hip. The music grew closer, and now the voice was easier to understand. Ji whispered the words of the familiar song. "Beware the roaring onyx sky before it blazes red . . ."

As he crested the hill, Daeso met Ji's gaze and smiled. Ji blushed and turned away, focusing on the little one in her arms. She busied herself checking to make sure Jeul hadn't hurt herself when she bumped into Ji.

"Sibling dear,
I see you near.
You forgot your plight.
Remember that the day is short,
and you've no mom in sight."

Daeso continued improvising as he moved closer to Ji and Jeul.

"The night draws near,
but have no fear,
I promise you'll be
out of harm's way,
but I give no promises that you
won't go crazy by the end of the day."

Coming to a stop a couple of feet from the pair, Daeso bowed.

Jeul buried her face into Ji's neck. "See! I told you he was being mean."

"Daeso!" Ji chastised, though she struggled to keep a straight face. "You ought to be ashamed of yourself! You're scaring her."

"Well, someone's got to keep her the perfect little gem. No spoiled gems are allowed." Daeso swung the guitar to his back and began tickling Jeul, until she squirmed so much that Ji had to put her down.

"I'm telling Mom!" Jeul began weaving through the crowd.

Ji giggled as she watched Jeul go. When she turned back to Daeso, he was staring at her affectionately, which made her quickly look away again. Tucking her hair behind one ear and taking a deep breath, she slowly looked back at Daeso, who was now searching the crowd, most likely for his sister and mother. When Daeso turned his attention back to Ji, meeting her sky-blue eyes, they both smiled, their breath quickening.

"Well," Daeso finally said, "it's time to rally the masses."

Ji's smile disappeared, replaced with pursed lips and worry lines etched across her forehead. "You've got to be careful, Daeso! The two are watching, and they are not kind."

"The two . . . they . . ." Suddenly, Daeso's eyes were on fire with anger. He raised his voice as he responded. "They? Can we not say the brothers' names? We shouldn't have to fear some old men watching us from miles away on a mountain no one can climb. If it can't be climbed, then neither can they get to us."

"But the dragon," a man chimed in from the gathering crowd.

"The dragon, yes. If we grouped together instead of cowering in fear, we could fight the dragon! Together, we could eradicate our fear and be free again."

A woman in the crowd asked quietly, "And just how would you do that?"

Daeso pursed his lips. "I'm not sure, but we could make a plan."

Ji dropped her gaze to her feet. "Everyone who has ever tried to make a plan has been carried away by the dragon, though. And you would never be able make a plan in time to save everyone who agreed to be part of the plan either." A tear rolled down her face.

"Are we supposed to just sit here and allow it to happen, then?"

Daeso demanded. "Just cower in fear and let them continue their reign, leaving us only scraps of the food we labor to bring to life? No one should have to live in fear just because they're not privileged to be an Elder."

"You're scaring me." Ji sniffled and wiped her sleeve across her face. "No one has ever stood up to them and lived. Please don't try this."

"I refuse to live in fear of the Elders! Who's with me?" Daeso thrust his fist up high and scanned the crowd, which had begun to disperse. Shrugging, he sighed. "It was worth a shot."

"Maybe one day, Daeso, but not today." Ji grabbed his hand and pulled him behind one of the stands, where empty crates were stacked haphazardly. Daeso grabbed a crate for each of them, flipping them on their sides.

Unable to sit yet, Ji searched Daeso's face as he seated himself. "How are you so brave?"

"It isn't bravery; it's stupidity. At least, that's what my mom says." He chuckled. "But she also says we must stand up for what we believe in. I may not have much in the way of power or fighting skills, but I'll use what I have, even if that's only songs to inspire others."

"I don't know how you do it. I worry all the time." Ji stood stock-still, her eyes glued to the Elders' mountain.

"It's not that I don't worry! I worry all the time." Determination filled Daeso's voice. "But I would rather be afraid of the consequences of my actions than petty punishments that may come whether or not they're deserved. Can you imagine a land where we are free to feel what we want without punishment?"

His voice took on a mischievous tone. "Not to mention, who could be afraid of such wrinkly faces?"

Ji didn't laugh, her gaze still caught on the distant mountaintop.

Daeso sighed. "I'll be okay, you know. The Elders live way up there. How would they ever know? Not to mention, they've never come for anyone who wasn't of age. I'm safe!"

"Maybe." Ji allowed herself one last fervent glance at the mountaintop where the Elders lived, lording over the village, and took a deep breath. "But please wear this." She took a bracelet with a single smoky quartz from around her wrist and dropped it into Daeso's hands, cupping them between her own. "It's known to provide the wearer invisibility. Maybe it will be enough." She bit her bottom lip for a moment before standing suddenly. "I've got to go." She let go of his hands and walked away determinedly.

"See you tomorrow?" Daeso called after her, but she did not look back.

Daeso and Jeul were still in the market when a large shadow loomed over the village a few hours later, circling on widespread wings. The village bell rang out, signaling for everyone to hide from the familiar sight as quietly as possible.

A mighty fire cut across the sky, lighting up the bright green scales of the dragon's underbelly. The temperature quickly rose with that solitary breath, but Daeso and Jeul shivered where they crouched nonetheless.

The ground shook as the dragon landed in the middle of the village, accompanied by the scream of a single child, though the sound was quickly cut short.

The dragon didn't speak aloud. Instead, her thoughts filled Daeso's mind, and he knew the other villagers could hear them as well. *I am Yong, dragon of the Elders, destroyer of lawbreakers. Come to your fate, Daeso Orobu!*

Jeul clutched Daeso's hand, her eyes wide and pleading. As Daeso worked to gently remove his hand from her firm grasp, he whispered, "It's okay. It will be okay." Once free, he quickly kissed her forehead. "Stay hidden, all right?"

Jeul nodded, tears welling in her eyes.

Daeso held his breath as he stepped out from behind the market stand they'd used for cover. He tried to shift his guitar to his back nonchalantly as he stumbled into the murky smoke that the dragon's nostrils continually released. The dragon's tail nearly knocked him over as it swept past him, and he wondered if the dragon could see him any better than he could see her.

"Daeso, the Elders have ruled your insubordination intolerable. Your punishment: death."

A moment later, the dragon took flight once more. Circling the village, Yong sent out one last thought: *"Let this be a warning to you all."*

Daeso landed, soaked, on a cave floor and watched as the dragon's tongue withdrew into her mouth. With his guitar still strapped to his back, Daeso stared wide-eyed at his captor, afraid to move. Yong returned the stare, but her sky-blue eyes seemed only curious.

Suddenly, Yong raised her head and blew out a stream of fire. Expecting to be engulfed in flames, Daeso cringed and curled in on himself.

When all he felt was warmth and the vibrations of Yong walking farther into the cave, Daeso peeked out. The cave now glowed with blue flickering light, which emanated gently from a large crystal at the top of the cave. Tiny crystals reflected the new light all around them.

Hesitantly, Daeso inched toward Yong, who had turned around to watch him. Against his own wishes, he began to admire the cave's beauty and how the contained flame made Yong's scales glow.

Finding courage, he said, "Mighty Yong, I can see why you live in this cave; it is a natural treasure."

A low, rumbling chuckle filled the cave, as well as smoke that Yong couldn't hold in.

"Oh," Daeso said, suddenly worried, "dragon's do hoard treasure, right?"

"Yes. But crystals are no treasure to me."

"Then what is your treasure?" Daeso peered into the darkness of the cave.

"My treasure is right in front of me. You are a treasure."

Now it was Daeso's turn to laugh.

"You radiate the desire to help others through song . . . even though it almost meant your death."

More comfortable now, Daeso began to look at Yong differently. He observed her quietly and noticed for the first time how beautiful she was. He reached out, almost touching her. "May I?"

"You may."

He gently caressed her wing as she watched. A warm sigh escaped the dragon, and she seemed to relax. Smiling, Daeso looked more closely at the scales beneath his hands. Soon, his eyebrows knitted together.

"You've been hurt! Many of your scales are broken, with scars in their place."

"Yes." Yong looked away and laid down, but not before Daeso spotted the pain in her eyes.

"Who hurt you?"

Instead of answering, Yong laid her head down and closed her eyes.

"But you are the mightiest in the land."

"Those were just children's stories the Elders created to scare your people."

The hair at the nape of Daeso's neck stood on end. "The Elders?"

"Yes."

He gently traced a deep scar, and anger filled him. "The Elders?"

"Yes."

"But you could fight them!" he said, perplexed. "How could such a strong dragon be hurt by any human, even Elders?"

"I've never had a choice. I was born and raised by the Elders, like my mother before me." Yong yawned. *"Enough of that for tonight, though. We are safe here, and I am tired. Let us rest."*

Daeso yawned largely, suddenly realizing just how tired he was.

"Come." Yong raised one wing.

Daeso hesitated, worried about his future and what would happen to his mom and sister without him, but fatigue was overwhelming the desire for answers and the drive to convince Yong to fight the Elders. Leaning his guitar on the wall, he laid down beside Yong.

"Sweet dreams," he said as Yong's wing curled around him.

The sunrise shone on Daeso as he quietly strummed his guitar, his legs hanging over the cliff's edge.

"*Daeso?*" Yong called.

"Out here."

Daeso continued strumming as Yong approached. "*What are you doing?*"

Daeso pulled his legs up from over the ledge and sat cross-legged facing Yong. "I've just been playing and thinking."

"*What about?*"

"You, mostly." He hesitated. "I even started writing a song about you. Is that okay?"

"*A song about me?*"

"Yeah, the real you. Not the scary, fictional tale. Want to hear it?"

"*Yes, please.*"

"Beautiful as emeralds, scales and kindness shine. . . . That's all I have so far. What do you think?"

"*Your voice is beautiful, as I already knew, so of course your song is too.*" Yong hesitated, then added, "*I have a confession to make. Wait right here, and I will be right back.*"

Daeso nodded and went back to strumming his guitar as he tried to further describe his new scaly muse.

A few moments later, a nervous voice called out. "Daeso?"

Daeso turned his head to find a familiar young woman standing in the cave entrance. He immediately scrambled to his feet, leaving the guitar at the cliff's edge. "Ji!" He smiled widely. "When did you get here? I didn't see you last night. Where did you sleep? Are there others?"

Ji's sky-blue eyes widened. "Whoa, hold up! I can't answer so many questions at once."

Daeso pulled her into a hug. "It's so nice to see you!"

"Thanks," she said shyly.

As they pulled away, Ji began playing with a chain around her neck. A unique half-moon pendant fell out from behind her collar.

"I don't think I've seen that before." Daeso reached out to touch the necklace. "Is it part of a real dragon scale? Was it a gift from Yong?"

Ji started and quickly tucked the pendant away in her shirt. "Oh . . . that? My mom gave it to me before she died."

"Oh, I'm sorry! At least you have something to remember her by."

"Yeah." Ji looked away, her hand once again caressing the necklace's chain.

"Was she a victim of the Elders?" Daeso asked, though he quickly regretted it. "You don't need to answer if you don't want to."

"Yes," Ji whispered, almost inaudibly.

They both stayed silent for a few moments.

After a while, Daeso realized the dragon hadn't returned, so he began walking into the cave. "Yong, where did you go?" Turning to Ji, he said, "She wasn't going to be long. She said she had a confession to make." He turned back to the cave. "Yon—"

Ji tapped him on the arm.

When he turned to her, she gave a small wave and smiled apologetically. He gaped as realization struck.

"But . . . you can't . . ." He began pacing, trying to wrap his head around the idea. After a long struggle, he added, "Can you?"

"Yes. I am both Yong the Mighty and Ji from the market."

Silence fell again, and Daeso watched as Ji sat at the cliff's edge, kicking her dangling feet. "Ji? Yong?" He sat beside her. "Ji-Yong." He smiled at her, nodding in acceptance.

"Y-you're okay with this?" Ji asked, her eyes on her dancing feet.

"Of course. No matter what your form, you have always been my friend and shown me kindness, and I'll always do the same for you." He reached over and clasped her hand.

They spent the rest of the day catching up on the cliff's edge, gathering supplies for their new cave home, and answering Daeso's questions.

"Was your mother the first?" Daeso asked as they gathered wood for a fire. "The story they tell us says the Elders fought a dragon with their magic, hurting it just enough to take control of it. They brought the dragon to what is now the Elders' mountain and took control of its mind, forcing it to terrorize the village so the villagers would provide for their needs."

"If what I have heard is true, they found my mother's egg before she was ever born. They improved their magic using the magic radiating from her, even when she was still inside the shell. We've never even known what freedom was. Elder Olae likes to throw it in my face that they use my own magic against me."

Ji looked down at the branches in her arms, tracing a line of bark with her finger.

Daeso inhaled sharply. "Wait, do they control you mentally?"

"Um . . . it isn't mind control exactly. They can read my thoughts if I'm near them. They can cause major pain in my head and control my body if they are close. Their punishments are severe for insubordination, as you and all the Elders' victims know." She slowly took in a deep breath and held it.

Daeso reached out and gripped her hand. "You're one of those victims too." His thumb stroked a scar on the top of Ji's hand. Ji placed her head on Daeso's shoulder and sighed. This was how they stayed as they watched the sun set and green flickers of light reflect from Ji's sweater.

Later that evening, as they ate some berries they had gathered, Daeso abruptly interrupted their conversation with a jubilant yell. "I've got it! Listen:

"Beautiful as emeralds
Scales and kindness shine.
Ji-Yong fought the Elders
Who thought they were divine."

Daeso laughed. "Eh . . . maybe not. That sounded better in my head."

Ji frowned. "I haven't fought the Elders anyhow."

"Well, you saved me, and that was against their wishes, right?"

"Y-yes, but if they find out, I'll be punished severely." Her eyes suddenly widened. "Thanks for the reminder, though. I must go."

"But what about me?"

"I know you. You'll be able to survive, but be careful and stay in the cave. As you know, the cave isn't accessible to men." She hugged him tightly and began to run toward the cave's mouth, then abruptly turned around and came back. "I want you to have this." She removed her necklace and put it around his neck.

"But it's your mother's! I couldn't!"

"You will, and it isn't just a necklace. If you need me, rub the half-moon dragon scale pendant and think my name." She gave Daeso a quick kiss on the cheek, then ran toward the cliff's edge, her body expanding into her dragon form. She leaped off the cliff and dropped as her body finished taking shape.

The last Daeso saw of her, she was still flying in spirals, mimicking the feeling in his stomach.

"Ji-Yong?"

"Yes?"

"Thanks."

There was a pause before Yong warmly replied, *"It is my pleasure."*

Arriving at the Elders' vantage point atop their snowy mountain, Yong landed quickly and bowed.

The crouched figure of a white-robed Elder almost blended into the mountainside. *"Trouble—that should have been your name. You were supposed to come here immediately after eating the boy."*

Elder Olae's voice cut painfully through Yong's head. Part of her wanted to just eat them, set them on fire, or worse to punish them, but she was too familiar with the screaming pain they could inflict within her head and upon her body.

As a whip came down upon her side, Yong gritted her teeth and tried hard to contain her tears, knowing they would only make the punishment worse.

"Daydreaming again. Another infraction." Elder Doen turned to their servant, Doum, and added aloud, "Add another fifty lashes to the punishment."

Doum, who had been administering the punishment, hesitated,

pushing her glasses up her nose. "That would be one hundred total, right, Elder Doen?"

"Yes, Doum, and I better see welts for all one hundred lashes, or you'll receive more lashes yourself. And most of them better be bleeding!"

Doum bowed her head as the Elders began to leave.

"And if she cries," Elder Doen added offhandedly, "add fifty more."

Once the Elders were out of sight, Doum whispered, "I'm sorry." Yong let the tears flow.

By the time Doum left, Yong was too exhausted to move. That night, she slept exposed to the snow and cold winds, numb to everything but physical and emotional pain.

The next morning, Ji was back in human form, observing the village through a magical frozen pond atop the Elders' mountain, where she had been magically bound as her injuries healed. The beautiful colors of the village stood out against the mountaintop, distracting her from the pain of her rapid healing.

As her eyes settled on the spot where she had picked up Daeso, she wondered how he was doing in her absence.

"Ji-Yong?" Daeso's voice rang through her mind.

"Daeso?"

"Are you okay? I haven't been able to reach you."

Ji tried to hold back tears in case one of the Elders appeared. *"I'm sorry! I must have been too hurt to hear you."*

"Hurt? Oh no, did you have an accident?"

"No. It . . . I . . ."

"It was the Elders, wasn't it?" Daeso's concern had morphed into outrage.

Ji didn't respond as memories flooded her mind.

"Oh, Ji-Yong! I'm so sorry!"

Ji immediately attempted to clear her mind. *"I didn't mean for you to see that. I'm still not in full control of my emotions. I apologize."*

"You apologize? They're the ones who should be apologizing!"

"I will be okay. I've had worse."

"You must fight back. You can't let them control you like this."

Ji knew Daeso was right, but . . .

"I can't."

"Why not?"

"You wouldn't understand."

"Try me."

"This is the only life I have ever known. What if it's too hard on my own? I'm not ready."

"I know new is hard." A flood of images poured into Ji's mind. She saw Daeso's memory of looking up at her in dragon form as the smoke swirled around them before she swept him away. She felt the shivering cold in his hands as he tried to make a fire alone in their dark cave, and she saw the sparkle of crystals reflecting the fire throughout the cave. *"But you won't be alone. I promise!"*

"You forgive me for leaving you alone there?"

"Well, I would prefer to vacation with you, but I've made do." They both giggled, though Ji's was nearly silent for fear of being overheard.

"Another must be punished!"

Elder Olae's sudden intrusion shocked Ji from her amusement, and she immediately blocked her connection with Daeso. "Y-yes, sir."

"Actually, make that two. Usually, I do not condone the death of children, but from such a troublemaking family, there is no doubt the youngest would turn out the same." The Elder walked around Ji to stand directly in front of her.

"A child?"

Elder Olae cocked one eyebrow. "You dare question me?"

"No, Elder Olae." She bowed, making sure her gasps of pain weren't audible.

"Good. You better not run off like you did last time."

"Yes, sir. I'm sorry I disappointed you, sir!"

She kept her head low and pushed her magic to quicken her healing. Lost in thought and pain, she didn't hear the list of broken laws, real or imagined, that Elder Olae recited.

". . . Omma and Jeul Orobu."

Elder Olae's final words cut through Ji's distraction, and she faltered. Shock broke through the barrier separating her from Daeso and reverberated through her head. Hoping to distract the Elder in case he was monitoring her mind, she quickly said, "That is the family of the last sinner, right?"

"How charming," Elder Doen chimed in as he ascended the steps behind Ji. "Yong remembers the names of her victims. That should make finding the rest of the family that much easier. Now go!" With a snap of his fingers, the magical restraints released Ji.

She changed forms and took off, diving off the mountain to put as much distance between her and the Elders as quickly as possible before leveling off. She'd left without answering, too afraid she'd betray Daeso or her own thoughts. Her desire to save Daeso's family drove her forward, and she ignored the pain that came with every flap of her wings.

As she circled the village, she formed a plan.

Landing and surrounding herself with thick smoke, she called forth the Orobu family. Once they were outside, she directed her thoughts to their minds only.

"Please trust me. Climb upon my back as quickly as you can."

Omma and Jeul Orobu climbed onto the dragon's back under the cover of smoke Yong had created. Once they were settled, Omma gently patted Yong's side, and Yong took off without delay, flying toward her cave, in the opposite direction of the Elders' mountain.

Once distant enough from both the village and the Elders' mountain, Yong allowed Daeso's anxious thoughts to pass through the barrier she'd thrown up, sharing the connection with the pair on her back.

"Are they okay? What's going on?"

"Daeso?" Jeul called out.

Omma nodded and whispered a confirmation in her ear.

"Yes, and we'll see you soon," Yong replied. Omma and Jeul laid flat against Yong's back as the dragon flew toward her cave as quickly as she dared with her precious cargo.

Once Yong reached the cave, she landed as quickly yet safely as possible. Daeso ran out of the cave to help his family down.

Once on the ground, Jeul hugged Yong's front leg tightly. "I knew the rumors weren't true. I told you, Daeso."

Yong bowed her head. *"I am not without shame for my past actions."*

Omma gently stroked Yong's scales. "No one is without fault, Yong. What matters is how you continue to learn, grow, and try your best with that knowledge."

"But it's hard not knowing what will happen as a result."

"That's true, but no one expects perfection from you—"

"The Elders do."

"No one who truly cares about you would expect it. If you try your best to do the correct thing and keep an open mind so you can learn from any new information, then you are on the right track."

"Thank you." Ji turned her attention to Daeso. *"Do you still have the smoky quartz bracelet I gave you?"*

He nodded, showing his wrist and the bracelet encircling it.

"Stay together. That bracelet will protect you from their sight. I hate to run, but I better not keep them waiting."

Yong bowed her head as Daeso and his family waved goodbye. As the distance grew between them, the truth of Omma's statement reverberated through Yong, empowering her.

When Yong landed before the Elders, she stood tall, refusing to cringe as Elder Olae's voice cut through her mind.

"I will not bow any longer, and I beg you to change your ways."

Her words were met with a lashing. She lowered her head to meet Doum's eye.

"Join me, please. Do not let them control you any longer."

Doum looked back and forth from the Elders to the whip in her hand. Lifting her chin defiantly, she dropped the whip and quickly moved behind the now-brazen dragon.

"Have you forgotten you have no other home?" Elder Doen demanded.

"If you can call this a home." Daeso's voice rang out in Yong's mind, emboldening her further.

Elder Doen called the whip to him with his magic and attempted to punish Yong. Realizing his intention, Yong stood on her hind legs and flapped her wings forcefully. A spell crackled around Elder Doen's hand and the whip, but the wind Yong generated slammed the Elder against the mountainside, where he dropped to the ground, motionless.

"Sorry! That was a little more forceful than I intended." Regardless of the pain the Elders had caused, Yong couldn't forget the bond they'd shared since her birth.

"You will be sorry." Yong winced as Elder Olae's voice lashed against her mind.

"Remember: you are strong and powerful." Omma's voice brought Yong renewed purpose and strength.

Yong whipped around to find Elder Olae holding a red-faced Doum a couple of feet off the ground in a chokehold of magic. *"Don't do anything rash, Yong,"* he commanded.

"No, I can't stand by and let you abuse your power! You will be stopped. Today!"

Elder Olae gaped up at Yong for a moment, but he soon took a deep breath and held his head high. *"You must learn your place! You belong to me!"*

"You will not hold power over anyone ever again!"

Yong flew straight up in the air. The sky, dark with thick storm clouds and smoke, lit up around her as lightning crackled. The dragon roared loudly into the night, and with blinding anger, flame erupted forth.

Elder Olae fell backward, losing his magical hold on Doum, who quickly slipped away. The heat of the night drew sweat from Elder Olae, but he got back to his feet.

"You think you can be free? So did your mother, but you've seen where that got her."

Yong looked to the edge of the Elders' mountaintop, where a

defiled skeleton hung. Long before her birth, it had fed the power-hungry Elders.

"Once she knew you were soon to be born, she, too, thought she could get the upper hand. She forgot her place, just as you do now."

Crackling magic in the form of a whip began to wrap around Yong's neck, pulling her from her distraction and causing her to lose altitude.

Seeing red, Yong made a choice to use her magic to harm instead of help—something she had only done previously when under duress. Her mind reeled with all the ways the Elders had abused her magic, pooling it for nefarious purposes: To spy upon the villagers, to control her, to live beyond their years.

To kill her mother.

Elder Olae spun high in the air, lofted by Yong's magic. His wrinkled face turned red, his eyes wide and his mouth gaping. He flipped head over heels, ever higher, until he looked like a rag doll, his limbs and head flopping and sagging in the arching whirl.

Omma's voice rang in Yong's mind. *"Yong? Yong! Can you hear me?"*

"What?" Yong growled back.

"Thank goodness you can still hear us!"

"What do you want?" Yong watched the arching progress of her prey.

"Is this really what you want?" the thoughts of all three Orobus asked at once. Their faces flashed in Yong's mind. Suddenly, worry over her decisions began to eat into her anger and frustration. She watched as Elder Olae began to descend, his fall uncontrolled now that she'd stopped using her magic.

Yong shot into the air and opened her mouth wide.

Yong descended upon the village and spat Elder Olae out onto the ground in front of the village jail. Doum dismounted and untied the ropes holding the unconscious Elder Doen to Yong's side.

Doum spoke with an officer to explain what was happening and their need for more restraints. While Doum worked to secure the unconscious Elders, the officer ran to tell anyone who would listen about the Elders' being brought to the jail by Yong the Mighty.

Soon, villagers began to appear, nervously standing at a distance, until the Elders were secured and the villagers knew nothing was going to happen to them. Only then did one of the villagers yell out, which started an avalanche of anger and frustration. The villagers quickly became a crowd, jeering and shouting and encircling the front of the jail as they called for justice.

Yong roared loudly, quieting the crowd. *"I understand your anger and desire for justice, but their deaths will not avenge the decades of torture and power these brothers have held over all of us."*

"How would you know? You were in league with them," one villager yelled.

"She was forced by the Elders to do those things," Doum called, stepping out in front of Yong. Murmurs filled the crowd as they tried to figure out Doum's role in the matter.

"Both of you deserve to die, just like them," a new voice yelled from the crowd.

"I understand how you might have come to such a conclusion, but we are all on the same side. All of us have been wronged, but dwelling in that anger will only produce more anger, just like obsessing on fear only creates more fear. We must break the cycle, overcome, and start afresh, learning from the mistakes of the past."

Before their eyes, Yong became Ji. "Many of you know me and have trusted my advice in this form, so I beg you: Look within your hearts to find calm in this storm of anger. Find strength in knowing that wrongs will be righted, and know that true change takes time and commitment, not riotous public executions."

A young mother stepped forward, holding a child who wore a bracelet with a sparkling rainbow moonstone. "I trust her."

A man with an onyx necklace joined her. "I do too." He removed the necklace from around his neck and placed it in Ji's hand, bowing his head as he backed away.

"Thank you." Ji put the necklace on and stood taller, more confident.

Many others came forth, each bearing their own story of how Ji had helped them or their family. They began to form a protective ring around Ji.

When the Elders began to regain consciousness, Ji motioned for the crowd to back away and shifted into her dragon form, drawing gasps from the villagers.

"Elder Doen, Elder Olae," Yong said, allowing her thoughts to echo loudly in everyone's mind. *"The villagers, the rightful owners of this land, have ruled your insubordination intolerable. Your punishment . . ."*

Yong stared hard at the Elders. She wasn't sure if she would be successful, but she knew she had to try.

"Your punishment: removal of your magic."

Sparks of magic crackled and encircled the Elders in a whirlwind of colors, and with a deep inhalation, Yong sucked the magic in. After several deep breaths, Yong's eyes filled with bolts of magic that then calmed with every breath.

Doum stepped forward and pulled a necklace bearing a piece of Yong's green scales from each of the Elders' necks. "Including these." Doum stepped back into the crowd, who cheered. The officers of the village stepped forward and prodded the Elders to their feet, walking them into their new home. They closed their barred cells with confidence, knowing the Elders would never be able to retaliate.

Doum and a couple of trusted villagers stationed themselves in front of the jail to ensure no harm came to the new occupants. Yong flew off to retrieve the Orobu family, who had helped her find herself and the name she would forever be known by, regardless of her form: Ji-Yong.

"Floating emerald savior,
Her scales and kindness shine.
Beware, the power hungry,
For your reign you will resign."

Ji-Yong gently shoved Daeso's shoulder. "Really?"

"It's better than 'She will turn you into swine.'" Jeul could barely speak through her giggles.

"I'll get it. Just you wait." Abruptly, Daeso gave a cry of triumph. "I have it! 'Do not dare to cross the line.' How about that?"

Ji-Yong shook her head, a wide smile on her face. Her belly hurt from laughing too hard.

She knew everything wouldn't magically fix itself, but she also knew she was enjoying this new chapter of her life.

A Dark and Terrible Beauty

K. A. Moore

The door creaked open. Jemma huddled into the corner, and rough wood scraped against her, digging splinters into skin. Anemic light seeped through the porthole, providing no warmth to her nakedness. Her dress lay shredded on the filthy floor. She peered through matted curls as boots stepped over piles of urine and feces where Jemma had had no choice but to relieve herself. As the boots drew closer, Jemma curled more tightly into herself.

"My God, it smells bloody awful in here," said a voice above Jemma; the boots had stopped inches from her. "What pigeon-livered blockhead put you in conditions like this? And without a chamber pot, no less, or adequate clothing? The captain won't like this."

Straw crunched to Jemma's left, and a warm hand touched her shoulder. Jemma pressed herself to the wall, flinching away from what she knew came next. She heard a sigh and a crunch as they stepped back.

"You don't have to be afraid; I'm here to rescue you. I promise I won't hurt you." A tug at her scalp and the whisper of cloth as the newcomer crouched down were the only things keeping the dizziness at bay. "Only a few more. Sorry about the tugs, but it can't be helped. Ah, there we go."

Face now clear, Jemma looked into the bright eyes of the person before her. Delicate features blurred for a moment before coming into focus.

"You're female," Jemma rasped out, like rust cracking from old door hinges.

"Of course I am. Why do you think—" The young woman stopped, realization sparking in her eyes. "Oh."

A wave of dizziness had Jemma slumping to the floor. The girl rushed to help her sit up. "You're safe now. Let me go get help."

"No!" Jemma gripped her savior's wrist with the last of her strength. "Don't leave me. I don't want to be alone again."

Warmth settled over Jemma. "Don't worry. I won't let anything more happen to you." A pause. "You know, this would be easier if I knew your name."

"It's Jemma." Black dots appeared at the edges of her sight, and her stomach roiled.

"Jemma. You can call me Sam."

Jemma vomited, and her world went black.

Jemma woke on a soft bed. As she took in her surroundings, her eyes landed on a man sitting in a chair across the small room. A book lay open on his lap as he gazed out the window, unaware she had awakened.

Blackbeard.

The last time she'd seen him, he'd disappeared into his cabin while his men dragged her onto this ship before she lapsed back into unconsciousness. How long had she waited for someone to rescue her before they made their grand entrance? The numbness that had seethed for so long faded, replaced by an icy rage.

"You!"

The captain's head snapped around toward her. She flung the blankets off and stood, swaying for a moment before crumpling to the ground.

He rushed over. "Are you all right?"

She pulled back. "Don't you dare touch me! You're responsible for this!" She struggled to pull herself up using the side of the bed, her arms shaking with the effort. "You should have killed me. It would have been a mercy compared to the hell you thrust upon me." She finally managed to sit on the edge of the bed, her chest heaving.

"There seems to be a misunderstanding."

She made an unladylike sound. "All is well, then. After all, it was just a misunderstanding."

He shot her a look that made her heart beat like a hummingbird's wings. "Check your tone, madam."

"Check my tone?" She rose and walked toward him on shaking legs, using the furniture for support. "My place was in London as a lady with a future. Now look at me!" She gestured toward a looking glass off to the side. Her reflection looked like a child playing dress-up. "What future do I have now? Your crew took everything from me, and your only concern is for my tone?"

"Yes, I take issue with your tone," he snarled. "I don't know whose ship you believe you were on, madam, but it was not mine. We happened upon a ship limping along and stopped to offer our assistance. When I realized exactly what sort of debauchery we'd stumbled upon, I acted immediately. While I enjoy the stolen trinket or two, I do not—nor will I ever—enjoy the flesh trade. It's been just under a month since we brought you aboard. We were uncertain you were going to make it."

"A month?" Jemma swayed, the color draining from her face. "I've been unconscious for a month?"

"Yes. I'm not sure whether it was because you were so malnourished when we brought you aboard or it was the trauma you were forced to endure, but you've not been lucid for more than a few minutes at a time. You don't remember anything after we found you?"

"No. I remember there was a girl who found me, but little else after that."

"Yes, that would be Sam. She was adamant she search the lower decks after we boarded the ship. You have her to thank for your rescue."

Jemma circled the chair supporting her and plopped down. "You sent a female alone into a den of debauchery? What is wrong with you, man?"

"As I said—"

"I don't care what you've said. You should take better care of the women aboard your ship. For you to put Sam at risk like that is incomprehensible!"

"I promise you, madam, she is hardly at risk for more than a splinter aboard my ship. She has been treated like a queen since she joined my crew, and I would never put her in a position she couldn't handle. Besides, Sam is her own creature and would have my bollocks if I babied her."

He turned his back to Jemma and gazed out at the ocean. "You have her to thank for your current state. She took it upon herself to bathe and clothe you. And when she told me of the horrible state she found you in,"—he turned back toward her—"I handled matters on your behalf. You will room with Sam, with the knowledge that the men responsible have paid for their crimes." A pause. "Sam tells me your name is Jemma—"

"Jem. Jemma no longer exists; those men made sure of that."

He cleared his throat. "Jem, then. As you may already be aware, the men call me Blackbeard; you may do so as well."

"You said you handled things on my behalf. What exactly does that mean?"

His gaze burned into hers. "I killed them. All but one."

"All but one? Why even leave the one? You claim to not deal in flesh, but you left the one alive. Why? What sort of ship do you run here, Captain?"

"Do you think I'm feared merely by my looks? No, madam, I am feared because I take no prisoners. Since it has worked thus far, I see no reason to question it. I left the one man alive as a warning, and that only if he doesn't succumb to his wounds before anyone finds him."

"A warning?"

"Yes, a warning. A warning that anyone who dares attempt such a thing on my seas again will suffer the fate of his former crew."

"I can't believe you would let any stay alive. You should have killed them all."

"You go too far."

"You didn't go far enough! You shouldn't rest until they are all dead. I know I won't." Jem stood on shaky legs. "Now if you please, I would like to be alone. I'm tired and would like to rest."

"Of course. I'll call for Sam." He walked to one wall and pulled a string, ringing a bell farther in the bowels of the ship. "I hope you find your accommodations adequate. Hopefully, we can find a town or port that interests you."

"I doubt anything other than death would hold interest for me now, but I shall take all offers into consideration should the time come."

Sam walked through the door and made her way to Jem. Slipping her arm around Jem's waist, Sam glanced at the captain before giving Jem her full attention. "Would you let me help you to the bed? We wouldn't want you to hurt yourself."

"O-of course. Thank you, Sam."

"You're most welcome, Jemma."

Jem flinched. "Only Jem, please."

Casting one last glance at the captain, Sam led Jem toward their room as the door snicked shut behind them.

Jem jerked awake, dragging gulps of air into her lungs, and scanned the darkness. Something scratched against her skin, pawing at her roughly. She had to get away, had to—

She slammed to the floor in a tangle of blankets, her knees screaming in protest as they smacked into the hardwood. She scrambled on hands and knees to the other side of the cabin, hardly making it to the chamber pot. She heaved up the contents of her stomach, shuddering as she retched again and again, until only choking sobs remained.

She'd survived, *damn it*. Sam had saved her from hell in the bowels of that ship, and she wouldn't let these dreams drag her back. Her hands shook against the porcelain as she spat into the small pot.

She sat back against the wall, closing her eyes against the night sky beyond the window. She relished the coolness chilling the sweat on her skin, anchoring her further into the present and out of her nightmare-fueled haze. Her hands trembled as she dragged them through her curls, pushing the tangled mess from her eyes. Tremors racked her body, and she pushed herself harder into the wood, letting the weathered planks ground her to the present.

Anything to wipe the images from her mind.

The floorboards moaned as the ship rocked on the waves, echoing the screams from her nightmare. She held her breath, listening for any who might have heard her retching, but there were no footsteps or murmured conversations. Only the creak of the rigging and the moans of the ship as it shifted on the waves.

She'd rested her head but a moment when she felt the softest touch on her shoulder. Her eyes shot open to see Sam crouched before her, her brown eyes wide with concern.

"It's all right, Jem." Sam lifted a hand to cup Jem's cheek, and Jem leaned into the touch—the first that didn't send her seeking the chamber pot.

"Another bad dream. I'll go back to my bed in a few moments." She tried to smile, but her lips hardly lifted.

"Are you sure you'd rather stay aboard than go back to the mainland?" At Jem's dead look, Sam sighed. "Why don't you come sleep with me? It's been weeks of you fighting alone. It might help to have a friend beside you."

"I couldn't—"

"Nonsense." Sam stood, her hand outstretched toward Jem. "Come on."

Jem took her hand and followed her to Sam's bed. Motioning for her to go first, Sam climbed in as Jem slid to the far side of the bed. Wrapping Jem in her arms, Sam covered them with her small blanket.

In minutes, Sam's breathing had slowed. Jem watched the breath move through her lips for a few heartbeats before leaning forward and kissing Sam. As she jerked back, Sam's eyes opened and blinked at her. Jem held her breath.

"Why did you kiss me?"

Jem struggled to get up. "I'm sorry. I shouldn't have done that."

"Wait." Clutching Jem's arm, Sam tugged her back down. "You don't have to apologize. I only wondered why you did it; it didn't disgust me."

"I—"

"Jem, there are no secrets between us now; you can tell me anything."

Jem stilled and looked down. "I don't know what came over me. I felt in my soul that I would regret it if I didn't kiss you."

Sam cupped Jem's face in her hands. "Then why did you stop?"

Leaning forward, Sam pressed her lips to Jem's questioningly. Jem snaked her hand around the back of Sam's neck and pressed their lips harder together, as though her next breath wouldn't come if Sam's lips weren't on hers. The two tumbled together in a tangle of lips and teeth, letting their bodies do their talking. They kissed and touched until the sun rose and then fell asleep locked in each other's arms.

Weeks passed with Sam and Jem side by side, working for the captain during the day—though Jem avoided him whenever possible—and retreating to their quarters once the sun set.

Some nights, they'd sleep in each other's arms. On nights when the dreams became too much, Sam would touch Jem's body, spending long moments on the places most abused to remind Jem of the pleasure that could replace the memories that haunted her.

All the while, Jem felt unease rising within.

One week, she noticed a speck off in the distance, drawing closer with each gust of wind. On nights when even Sam's touch couldn't keep the demons at bay, Jem stayed on deck in a dark corner where she could go unnoticed. She would watch the spot where she last saw the speck, trying to see it through the darkness. Wondering what tidings would come once it drew close.

Every night, though, she made sure the knives Sam had gifted her were sharp in case someone made a move.

Black tendrils wrapped around the moon. The only light flickered from small flames in the deck lanterns. Most of the crew had gone belowdecks for a bit of drinking and gambling, leaving Jem and a few stragglers above deck. Perched atop a barrel, she ran her blade across a whetstone in rhythm to the waves slapping the ship. A stray curl had escaped the messy braid down her back to tickle her cheek. Raucous laughter carried over the sound of the harsh winds snapping the sails against their riggings.

The thump of footsteps grew closer to her, but it was only when the stench of body odor and horrid breath grew to be too much that she looked at the man.

"Well, what 'ave we 'ere? I bet ye thought ye were too good for us now that ole Blackbeard rescued ye an' keeps ye as 'is special pet." The man's yellow skin glowed in the dim light.

"Is there a particular reason you are over here, or am I to consider myself blessed to have my sense of smell as ruined as my maidenhead?"

He leaned closer, the stench wafting off his body enough to make anyone hurl. "I say we disappear belowdecks and ye let me show ye a better use for yer mouth than the shrewish words ye spew."

She stilled. "What did you say?"

"Ye heard me, wench. Do ye think jus' cos ye spread yer legs for the Cap'n in exchange for your rescue, he can prot—"

The whetstone clattered to the deck as she stood. The knife touched his throat like a lover's caress, opening the skin in mockery of a necklace. His eyes widened as he crumpled to the deck, his head smacking the weathered wood.

Jem stood over him. His mouth opened and closed as if he were a fish out of water. Each breath he took was shallower than the last.

"A much better use for *your* mouth, I daresay. Pity your useless carcass is making such a mess." She knelt so he could hear her above the cacophony around them. "I want my face to be the last thing you see. Remember this as you return to hell: there is nowhere on Earth or beyond where I won't find you. Death is only the beginning."

A final breath escaped his lips, and he didn't move again. His eyes stared at nothing as Jem stood. Wiping her blade on her breeches, she looked around for her whetstone.

She stopped as a sound caught her attention. Kneeling on the deck, she placed her ear to the wood and heard it a second time: the muffled scream of a girl. Jem jumped to her feet and raced belowdecks, searching each room she came to in the passageway. As she reached the final door, something pulled her back by the elbow.

"Don't go in thar; it's naught ye wish t' see."

Jem whipped around to face the interloper. "Do you think I care what I will see? There is a girl in there, and you do nothing! Remove your hand or lose it."

"Ye don't understand. It isn't—"

"What I understand is, you are a coward. You will unhand me at once, or I will make you."

The man released her arm and took a step back. "I didn't 'ave a choice but to give 'er to them. They made me take 'er—said it would be me 'and otherwise. If ye go in there, I won't be responsible fer what 'appens to ye."

"Who are *they*?"

"The men who jus' came aboard. They told me t' brin' 'em the lass, an' I thought they meant Sam."

"And for some godforsaken reason you thought it pertinent to give her over to some men without even informing the captain?"

"They threatened me 'and, mistress."

"You are one of the lowest life-forms I've ever had the misfortune to encounter." Jem shouldered past him to the door and tossed back over her shoulder, "You'll have more than your hand to worry about if you're still here when I return."

She shoved open the door and stopped in her tracks.

Lying in a heap between three men who were murmuring to one another, Sam stared at nothing, tearstains tracking through the dirt caking her face. With a gag shoved between her cracked lips, it was a wonder she could breathe. Jem would've come down whether the shouts she'd heard were male or female, but that it was Sam—*her Sam*—laid out on the floor about to suffer the same fate she had?

Jem saw red.

Hellfire spiraled through her body. Everything ached as ice became heat. Her daggers whispered against leather as she drew them from their sheaths.

On swift feet, Jem grabbed the closest man and shoved her blade through his back. Before the body hit the floor, Jem's second knife flew, hilt over blade, straight into the chest of her next target. The first knife, now free of the first man's back, carved its way across the throat of the third.

Jem panted as she slowed to a stop amid the bodies heaped around her. Sam huddled in a ball near the carnage. As if approaching an injured animal, Jem made her way over, crouching to Sam's level.

"It's all right, Sam. I've got you." Jem pulled the gag from Sam's mouth and sliced the ropes from her wrists.

Sam flung herself into Jem's arms, body shaking with the force of her tears. "I could have sworn no one could hear me, and they would— that they would—"

"Shush now." Jem squeezed her tighter. "No one is going to hurt you. Where can I take you to rest safely?"

Sam sniffled once more before pulling back. "Take me to the captain's quarters. I know I'll be safe there."

Pulling her upright, Jem walked her out of the hold. "For his sake, I hope so. If so much as one more hair of yours falls out of place, I'll gut him like I did these blokes."

They walked along in silence as they made their way above deck toward the captain's quarters. Jem flung open the door without so much as a knock and shuffled Sam inside. After settling Sam on the bed, Jem began opening drawers and cabinets, looking for weapons.

"What happened to Sam?"

Ignoring the man leaning against the doorframe, Jem kept looking, moving aside papers, maps, and books.

"I asked you a question, Jem. What happened to Sam?"

"She was attacked and requested to come here." Jem looked up from the drawer, her hand still searching, and leveled a glare at Blackbeard. "Now, if you would be so kind as to leave me alone, I'm looking for weapons."

He stepped into the room, his shadow looming over the mess she'd created. "And why, pray tell, do you need weapons?"

"Are you going to waste my time asking stupid questions, or are you going to help me?"

"I'm the captain here—"

"No! You don't get to pull rank on me, not now. One of your nitwit crewmen let several men aboard and practically threw Sam at them to save his own neck. If you—"

"What are you talking about, woman?" Blackbeard demanded. "What men?"

Jem stalked around the desk. "While you were off doing whatever it is you do to get your jollies off nowadays, some bloody idiot decided to not only let a band of men aboard but threw Sam to the wolves to save his own neck. Had I not heard her scream, Sam would have been much worse off. Now either tell me where I can find some weapons or get out of—"

"They're in the room next to the hold," Blackbeard answered, anger flashing through his eyes. "I make all the crew store their weapons there until we attack so there's no bloodshed if they get too deep in their cups. The key is in the top-left drawer under the false bottom."

He glanced back at Sam, his jaw firming. "I'll take Sam to a safe place. You grab the weapons, and I'll meet you on deck with the rest of the crew. No one boards my ship and attacks my crew and lives to tell the tale."

"And you think Jem fighting with the crew is a good idea? There isn't a way to keep her out of this?" Sam asked.

"Ha!" Jem slammed the desk drawer closed. "It's time someone showed them exactly why they shouldn't underestimate the fairer sex. I won't sit around like some damsel in distress waiting for someone to rescue me. Not only am I able to fight alongside the crew,"—she shoved past Blackbeard and through the door—"I will."

Jem headed back above deck, belt laden with weapons from the now-open storage. Two interlopers who had tried to stop her now lay in pools of their own urine and blood. Jem stalked across the deck, heading toward a group of men who had just climbed over the railing. At her approach, the man on the far side lifted his gaze.

"Wha' 'ave we here?"

"Come fer a wee taste, 'ave ye?" another chimed in.

"If ye're lookin' fer a taste, I 'ave somethin' fer ye t' choke on."

Only after the final man hit the ground did the shots register—along with the holes oozing blood right between each man's eyes. Like puppets on a string, the remaining men on deck looked up from their fallen friends to Jem, whose gun barrels still smoked.

"Anyone else have something crass to say, or can we start the real entertainment for the evening?" She met each man's gaze.

"Ye must be the wench Jack told us about. We've been lookin' fer ye." The man looked around at the others. "Looks like that fool gave our mates the wrong strumpet."

Jem dropped the guns and bowed, keeping her eyes locked on the men before her as she rose. "You've found me, but I'd watch who you call a strumpet."

"Wha' are ye yappin' about, wench? Our mate Jack can call ye whatever he wants. 'N' now he knows ye're still here, ye'll toe the line. 'Twill be a cold day in hell afore any more o' us die by yer hand."

Jem stared down each man, and when none so much as flinched, she threw her head back and laughed. "Do you feel that, boys? A cold snap is rolling in."

Before any of them could utter a word, Jem pulled a small throwing knife from her sleeve and flung it true—straight into the eye of the man closest to her, where the sleek wooden handle vibrated slightly.

A murderous cry went up from the men, but Jem smiled as if the devil himself had painted it there.

In a flash of steel, Jem had a sword in each hand, fending off each man's advance. The clang of metal rose over the waves, drowned out only by rumbling thunder. Sparks arced as blade struck blade, illuminating the bedlam and Jem's face for brief seconds. The metal sparked again, and the man before her stumbled back, his ruddy complexion paling.

"Y-yer eyes be red! Ye must be the daughter of Beelzebub himself!"

Jem ran her blade through his stomach, twisting the hilt as it rammed home. "It's an omen for where you're headed." She pulled her blade free, and his body dropped to the deck. "I'll see you in hell."

She didn't wait to see his last breath, only turned and took on the next man.

It could have taken minutes or hours. Each thrust and swing of her sword was like the tick of a clock. A parry here, her knife meeting flesh there. The only reason she knew it was still night was the darkness that crept toward blackness as the hour grew later.

And still she fought. It didn't matter that she faced fifty men. She fought through the fatigue when her sword arm drooped. She fought through the layers of fat and muscle as she thrust her knife through the gut of the closest target. She fought through the pain of her own wounds—mere cuts through her shirt, barely breaking the skin. She fought through her own fear, even as Blackbeard joined the fray with his crew and the face that haunted her nightmares flashed in and out among the men she fought.

As the numbers dwindled, so too did her strength, until only one man stood before her. The ragged scar across his right eye brought back the horrors of her time aboard the other ship. How she had screamed for help, to no avail. How she had tried to starve herself to end the agony of what they forced her through, night after night, for weeks.

Panting, she stared as he prowled closer.

"Looks like 'tis jus' th' two o' us, dearie. Blackbeard an' 'is crew be engaged with the fools I brought to keep 'is gaze from swingin' me way. Who would've thought such a scrawny witch like ye had some bite? How shall I make ye pay, then, hm? Shall I take the skin off yer bones like ye did these men, or shall I help ye remember jus' who ye're dealin' wit'?"

Rage seared her veins. "As if a lobcock like you would know the difference between a small hole and that nub between your legs."

"I'll show ye a nub, you foul-mouthed bitch."

"By all means." She threw her arms out in invitation. "If you think you're man enough, what are you waiting for?" He paused a moment and then lunged—only for Jem to catch his blade against her own. "So predictable, swine. Try to keep up, huh?"

"Ye wicked bitch, when I get hold o' ye, ye'll wish ye were dead."

"I'm already dead."

She pounced, sword outstretched in front of her, but he dodged, bringing his own sword down on hers.

They danced, trading blows, the only sound their heaving breaths and the sharp, metallic clang of their blades. When she got close enough, Jem used her knife to cut at him, but never enough to make it count as he moved out of reach.

Still they fought on. Jem's exhaustion cost her as her sword fell inch by inch. The man slipped past her guard, his sword cutting into her shoulder. With a yell, she stumbled back, dislodging the sword.

The sky chose that moment to open up, and rain poured from the heavens. Blood oozed from her wound, red droplets mixing with rain to collect in puddles on the deck.

Jem leaned against the rail, taking in gulps of air. Her breath hissed through her teeth as she fought through the pain. The man stalked closer, stopping a short distance from her—between her and her sword, which was discarded behind him.

He studied her for a moment and was opening his mouth to speak when she lunged. She plowed into his chest, rammed her shoulder into his gut, and turned to grab the sword in his hand. Wrestling it from his grasp, she jumped back and swung.

The blade arced high.

Metal tore through flesh, muscle, and bone, separating his head from the rest of his body. He hit the deck with a sickening thud that shook the deck.

Blackbeard stopped as the last enemy crewman fell and took in the carnage around him. Lightning danced through the clouds, illuminating the lone figure standing in the middle of the deck, chest heaving as rain soaked her through to the skin. He could make out each drop of blood as it mixed with rain, disappearing into her shirt. The blustery wind ripped the leather tie from her hair. Torn free of their braid and cascading around her face, her curls made her look like a dark, avenging angel.

Sword dangling from her hand, Jem looked over to him. "Now that I've solved your problem, get better lookouts when we make port." She swayed a bit. "And I would create a better alert system. I won't be here to clean up your messes forever."

She took one step and collapsed to the deck, her head rocking back and forth as if she were trying to get her world to stop spinning. A voice echoed over the waves breaking against the ship, calling her name.

"Sam," Jem whispered as she slipped into the waters of oblivion.

A Dragon's Hoard

JoAnne Turner

The golden warmth of the lamplight swayed with the ruts and bumps of the road, the hum of the carriage wheels, and the clop of the horses. The air was cool and smelled of the damp moor. It was the perfect conclusion to a glittering ball. Pity this last had been such a disappointment.

We were in a world of our own, headed to home and hearth. I shifted upon the richly upholstered carriage bench, rearranging Imaki in my lap and applying my handkerchief to the underside of a wing. The little dragon twitched her wing away.

"Hold still. You've a bit of a smudge here."

Really, though, she was almost perfect—smooth, leathery emerald skin without spot or blemish. My pale ball gown, high waisted with a golden gauze overlay and embroidered hem in the Egyptian style, had fared far worse in the dancing. I would never dance with half those partners again! Clumsy oafs had destroyed my hem. At least twelve inches and a flounce had torn right off, and the host hadn't even provided a ladies' receiving room for repairs. I had brought half a dozen extra gowns, plus coordinated accessories, in case of just such a disaster, and it had all gone to waste. It never would have happened during the season in London. I'd had to pin it as best I could and hold the rest up indecently high for the rest of the evening.

Still, beggars couldn't be choosers in Devon. In winter. After a week of sleeting rain.

Smudges cleaned, I folded my handkerchief back into my reticule. The bag's beaded fringe sent sparks of light dancing over the walls and ceiling of the carriage.

I trailed a finger down Imaki's neck and spine. She arched her neck and slit her eyes in pleasure. "You did such a good job this evening, especially with Lord Barttlelot's fairy preening and sparkling everywhere."

Imaki warmed to the compliment, snaking her tail around my wrist. "Lorelei's wings're prettier. Shiny and pearl."

"You should say, 'Lorelei's wings are prettier,' my dear, even though it's clearly not true. You are comparing elves and dwarves. Besides, it was Lord Barttlelot and Lorelei's ball. She is allowed to shine at her own ball."

And Imaki was a dragon. Always the superior choice. Not that I'd had to choose.

A snort sent a single spark arcing to the floor of the carriage. "Snooty, stuck-up princess. Should have contracted better."

"Lorelei or Lord Barttlelot?" I stomped out the spark with my slipper.

"Yes."

"Oh, hush." But I couldn't contain my own snort of laughter. "You need to be polite. Not everyone can be as lucky as you in their Fantastical Contract."

"Not a contract!"

I tapped a finger against her snout. "Yes, dear."

She grumbled but settled down on my lap for a snooze. I leaned back to enjoy the night. After a bit, Imaki's head bumped against my fingers, asking for a scratch or two.

Such a sweet girl. Almost home.

A shot rang out over the empty moor. The horses plunged and bolted. I threw up a hand to catch myself against the tilting of the carriage as my lanterns smashed to the floor.

Damn and blast!

Imaki tumbled nose over tail to the floor, hissing in outrage. Her talons tore at the upholstery as she clambered to the window, flame sparking deep in her throat.

"No, Imaki." I needed to think. Highwaymen? I sacrificed my cloak to smother the flames from the fallen lanterns, draping us in darkness. Had they hit my horses, or had Appleton merely whipped them into a frenzy?

"Thieves. Not safe. Steal the hoard." Imaki's gravelly voice was rising into fledgling registers, and little pools of yellow flame gathered in her chops.

Silly, impatient child.

I extracted the tiny dragon from the curtain, beating at the smoldering fabric and rubbing at her snout to remove any soot. Her eyes gleamed purple fire as she spiraled her serpentine body around my hand. I braced my foot against the opposite bench. The carriage was slowing as the driver got it under control. We didn't have much time.

"Gentle claws, dear. Watch the lace." I felt around for my reticule, straining to hear outside. Imaki must be hidden before we were overtaken.

"Need to protect the hoard." Her breath was all acrid smoke in my face, but her claws released their death grip on my palm.

Good. I'd have hated to resign them to the rag bin or, worse, give them to charity. These gloves were the finest Bulgarian lace.

The carriage jerked to the side, but I had braced well, and we remained upright. Two more shots, and we lurched to a stop. There were at least three more horses outside, judging by the snorting. Unshod and with very little tack. Or perhaps the men had wrapped all the metal to muffle the sound? Light from their torches illuminated the inside of the carriage just enough.

"You in the carriage. Out. Now." The voice was thick and wind roughened, with the stretched vowels of the local accent.

My questing hand finally found the silk of my reticule, and I shook it open, letting the torchlight catch the gleam within. Imaki fixated on that glint, pupils widening and neck ruff arching, but her tail still lashed with every bit of outside movement.

I pushed her at the opening, but her feet snagged on the edges of the fabric. "Dear one, you must get inside. Your hoard is here, and you can protect it all you want. Just hide, please."

"Exit now, or I'll have my men here start killing."

I shoved two fingers under Imaki's tail and scraped her off, glove and all, stuffing her into the reticule. Oh, to live back in the age when women could have pockets in their skirts! I yanked the strings shut with a whisper of silken rage. I'd even have settled for the last century, when I would have concealed the squirming bag in the deep folds falling from the hoops at my hips or the rolled pad at my rear. But ladies must be slaves to fashion, which meant high waists and straight skirts. I did my best to conceal Imaki among the filmy gold as the door was ripped open.

A hulking man filled the doorway, backlit by torches. There was something off about his hands or perhaps that graceful neck, but before I could study it more, he dragged me bodily from the coach. My feet tangled in my own torn hem, and I tottered like a month-old fledgling, all tail, neck, and ears. I hung by one arm from the giant's grip, trying to keep the reticule concealed in the folds of my dress, behind and away from the light. Imaki hissed, and I prayed that none of these dolts could hear.

Something pricked my side. Ah. He had a knife. Well, then.

I kicked my feet, trying to dislodge them from my torn hem. Cruel laughter echoed at my stumbles. My neck and ears burned with rage, but I refused to let the heat travel elsewhere. I was a lady. I could control myself.

I was surrounded by at least five men, including the clear leader in the center and Giant, who still held me. One wore an eyepatch and held a pistol on Appleton, still seated in the coachman's box. Another carried a torch in one hand and a pistol in the other. I couldn't see the fifth, but from the shifting of my carriage, he was atop. All of them were too poor for a pixie, their horses emaciated. They could have contracted with shy little brownies, but I doubted it. Only the unfit used the road for a living. Especially in the backcountry of Devon.

"What've we here, kiddies?" The leader was all glittering eyes and mocking smile. "A maid barely out of the schoolroom."

I warmed further at the malice in the leader's tone. He was short for a man, and he attempted to make up for it in swagger and the pistol at his belt. A rabbit trying to prove itself a fox. Didn't he realize both were prey?

That was a good name for him. Prey.

Gathering my feet underneath me, I used Giant's grip to stand. I turned my face to the wind, letting it cool the fire within me. Once I was certain I was chilled, I tilted my gaze up and to the left.

"Appleton?"

"Sweet as peaches, milady, don't you worry." My coachman's voice was tight but calm. "Knory's got the horses well in hand. Sorry we couldn't outrun 'em. Herded us straight to their friends here."

"Not your fault."

Knory bleated, and I could imagine the faun's hooves stamping in disgust. "Basic military strategy, and the sarge falls for it every time."

"Hey, I took the king's coin for twenty years—"

"Fifteen before you signed up with me, and how you stayed alive is—"

Gunshot.

I froze in the act of stuffing Imaki back in the carriage. Giant hauled me a step forward as everyone refocused on Prey. He held a smoking gun in the air.

He jerked his head at Eyepatch. "The fishwife and his cloven-headed pet don't seem to appreciate the situation. Remind them."

Eyepatch took one step closer to my coachman. My carriage. My horses. I let the rage lock my spine and spark in my eyes.

I tilted my chin at Prey. "My name is Lady Sofia Thistlewhite, my coachman is Mr. Appleton, his faun Knory. You will address me and mine with proper respect."

"'Ark at 'er, kiddies!" Prey blustered, every inch of him dripping disdain. "Brush off your company manners, lads. We got a lady in our midst."

The torchbearer bobbed his head with a grin that revealed all six of his teeth. I bit my tongue on the fury blazing in my throat. Gaptooth's hair would look so much better aflame.

"I'll be taking that flash at your neck and ears, my lady, if you please." Prey's tone held a whiff of menace.

"I do not please. You will have your man unhand me, and you will let us go." I fought to keep my free arm steady as Imaki jerked at my tone.

Giant's knife pressed into my side, threatening to rip my poor ball gown quite a bit higher than the previous tear. More ugly laughter echoed through the night. Prey's gaze flicked to Giant, who still held me fast.

"You hear that, Bess? She thinks you're a man!"

That's what had bothered me about Giant: no Adam's apple, and the hands were slender as a girl's. Still, for her size and clothing, it was an easy mistake to make.

"Stop playing with the lassie. We need to get gone." Giant's voice was lighter than I expected for one so large, a gentle burr of the far north. She was far from home. On the very edge of my hearing, she added, "And she had it right the first time, as well you know. Bastard."

Ah, not a woman in his soul, then. I smirked at the defiance in Giant's tone. I enjoyed spirit in my companions. Perhaps I would spare him from the coming blaze.

I gritted my teeth. There would be no blaze because I was a lady. I would handle this as a lady.

My trunk crashed to the ground, splintering and casting dresses, gloves, and bits of lace everywhere. All my beautiful things, strewn in the Devonshire mud. Prey toed at the spill of fabric and jerked his head at Gaptooth, who produced a sack more hole than fabric. I locked my jaw against a cry as the fine silks and velvets disappeared into the sack. This was going to be such an expensive evening.

My reticule whistled. Giant stiffened but kept an iron grip on my arm. Worse, Prey tilted his head in curiosity.

"My lady," Prey said, and gone was every bit of affability. "Show me your hands."

"Not a good idea." I twisted my arm in Giant's grip. "And seeing how your man here has a rather unkind grip on my arm, it is also not possible."

"Bess," Prey said with deliberate care, "let milady go."

The grip on my arm loosened, and I wrenched away, backing up against the carriage door to keep an eye on all the men.

"Thank you, . . . ?" I let my voice trail off, asking for a name.

"Just show your hands, dearie. None of this has to end in violence." Giant's voice was the toasty warmth of a gentle hearth, but his head hung apologetically.

I waited expectantly.

"It's Ben."

"Pleased to make your acquaintance, Master Ben." The rewards of politeness usually outweighed the annoyance. With Imaki still in my hand, I forwent the curtsy.

Smiling, I displayed my left hand, casually tucking my right into the carriage. Gaptooth glanced at me and paled. Hmm, perhaps there was a bit too much fang in my smile. I kept my head held high, shoved the reticule and Imaki under the carriage seat, and hoped the foolish child would stay quiet for once in her short life.

"Both hands, lass." Prey's eyes were quick and calculating.

I could almost see the piles of riches he was envisioning. Poor sweet thing. I was almost tempted to let him have his treasure. Everyone should dream of a hoard.

He grabbed Gaptooth's pistol and brought it to bear on me. The grinding click of him cocking it sparked in my ears.

On second thought.

I breathed in, enjoying the heat rising within me. It would be a good night to stretch. The tips of my fingers itched for the chance to return insult for insult.

But no. I clung to my breeding. The cool, moist air of the moor tamped down the spark of flame within me. Prey wanted both hands? I could give him that.

I splayed both hands in front of me: one gloved, one bare, both empty. The hissing behind me was reaching tea-kettle levels.

"The carriage." Prey waved the gun to force me to move.

I braced my feet, aiming an imperious nose at the little worm. Ben's mouth twisted in apology, even as he reached to haul me out of the way. I stepped right on my damned torn hem as I dodged, and sprawled full-out in the mud.

Imaki squealed in alarm at my shriek. Oh. Oh, this was awful. Cold, sticky red mud all down the front of my beautiful gown. It oozed between my fingers and up under my nails.

The last of the gang, the one who had been on top of the carriage, landed inches from my knee. He didn't even look at me as he reached into the carriage. His bald head shone with sweat as he fished out the smoking, squirming reticule, holding it by one string.

"Ah, that's the badger!" Triumph twisted Prey's mouth into an ugly sneer. "What do we have here?"

He stomped straight over a lavishly embroidered ball gown with three-quarter sleeves of fine lace. Mud bled into the delicate yellow satin, but I found I didn't care. All my senses were trained on my reticule, my heart held in shining silk. Imaki squawked as Prey grabbed the bag from Baldy's grip.

"Don't you dare!" Liquid fire rushed through my veins and propelled me out of the mud.

My precious little girl!

He was surely crushing her delicate wings. I would not let him harm her further. My throat burned and stretched wide, preparing to fight, as Prey tore at the ties and shoved a hand inside.

Then he was howling, waving his arm in the air. The cocked gun fired into the dark, and the flaming remnants of the reticule spun to the dirt. Imaki flapped frantically, spitting fire at Prey again.

"Imaki!" My relief at seeing her safe transmuted to dismay at the destruction. I stalked toward my errant dragon.

Imaki screeched her defiance and dove at Prey. "Took the hoard! Touched the hoard!"

"No more flaming! It's rude." I shook my finger under her nose. Bits of mud flicked into the night. Oh, dear. I peeled off the remnants of my soiled glove. "We'll both need a full wash when we get home."

Gaptooth beat at Prey's arm, dousing the fire. The flame snuffed out far too quickly. Pity. I could fix that. No one was even looking at me. They all had their gazes fixed on my little girl, who swooped around the flaming bag. Every single face was twisted with greed, and I shuddered to think what these men would do with her: Black market. Uncontracted partnerships. Cages and clipped wings.

I drew in a breath.

No. I was a lady, and I would handle this as a lady. I clung to the trappings of my rank with teeth and talons. My dress might be ruined. I might be covered in clinging, slimy mud. I might be a raging inferno within a thin shell of bitter ice. But there was no need to be rude. I drew in cool air to dampen the flame once more.

"What the hell is going on here?" That was Ben.

I looked back at him, jaw tight. "Never get between a dragon and her hoard."

He blinked at the crackling pile of former reticule. "What hoard? The little bit was stuffed in a bag."

Twitching my skirts out of the way and wrinkling my nose at the smell, I attempted to stomp out the last of the flames. Dance slippers were not meant for firefighting. Sighing, I fished Imaki's hoard from the flaming remnants and pinched it between two fingers.

No need to get it more soiled than it already was.

A handkerchief plucked from my poor pile of clothing served well to wipe the grime from my hands and Imaki's precious hoard. That done, I laid it flat on my palm—a single gold sovereign, shiny from constant rubbing against a dragon's scales. Imaki settled upon it immediately, scraping her chin along the edges and licking away at any soot.

"She's young. She has plenty of time to learn manners." I brushed at Imaki's scales, removing particles of ash.

Ice. I was ice.

I nuzzled her against my cheek. "But she's so darling, I find it hard to scold."

"That stupid spark-flare!" Prey snatched Imaki by the neck. "At least you'll bring in good money at the right market."

Imaki screeched, but she couldn't turn her head to get a good angle to fire. All the ice I had herded into my veins poured out in a rush. The world became darker and clearer as my eyes writhed through the shift.

"I wouldn't do that." Blood dripped from the punctures my nails had made in my palms.

"Because it's a tiny babber, still suckling mama's teat?" His hands tightened, shaking my precious girl. "I oughta snap her neck. Even the corpse can be sold for parts."

Bastard! As if Imaki were a piece at the auction of some sir who'd never been taught to properly hoard. And dragons don't suckle. They are fully functional from the moment they crack the egg. Unlike these useless humans.

"She's more valuable alive, boss," Ben said. He was giving me the strangest look.

Imaki whimpered, claws flexing. One thrash, but she couldn't get her claws around her wings to tear at her captor. Every movement was cut-crystal clear. The torch glowed white as color drained from the world.

"I would not do that if I were you." My chest was very full, near bursting from my stays as muscles shifted and flexed. "I like this dress, and it can still be saved with a thorough wash."

What could he see, with his tiny human eyes? Had he seen the scales creeping up my chest and over my neck? Could he tell my eyes had gone slit pupiled and lazy lidded, emerald fire banked in their depths? That my hair surged from its pins, flowing down to form a ruff on my neck? Surely he could see the way my bones shifted in my arms, bending them backward and up, membrane flowing between my fingers to catch the air.

"D'reckly, Ah'll take that dress too." Good Lord, his accent was getting worse by the minute. Prey wasn't even looking at me. He shook Imaki as a cat shakes a mouse and stretched out a hand to me. "Coin'll keep it calm?"

No matter. He would be able to see everything soon.

"The coin is Imaki's hoard." I raised my head, stretching out my neck. "But Imaki is the most precious treasure in mine."

I launched myself to the stars. My dress fluttered in the downdraft of my wingbeats. Four, five strokes, and I was high enough to wheel around and dive. The thieves' horses reared and bucked. A few sparks were enough to send the beasts screaming on their way. My own purebred stallions didn't even whicker, used to my antics and soothed by the expert hands of Appleton and Knory.

Such good boys. All of them.

Ben dived into the carriage, and Gaptooth, Eyepatch, and Baldy lay prone in the mud. My nostrils twitched. They had soiled themselves. No matter, they weren't the goal. I buffeted the air, prepping to land and knocking Prey over with a powerful gust. With deliberate precision, I settled my foot around Prey, claws digging into the mud at his shoulders, under his arms, and at that delicate place between his legs that men are so proud of.

Prey froze. I had to arch my neck and study him to make sure he was still breathing. It wouldn't do to end this too early.

Imaki settled between my shoulder blades, safe and warm. Her hoard was a cool spot on the first knob of my spine.

"All right, me luvver." My voice rumbled over the moor as I aped his accent. Ack, no. "We will discuss remuneration for the ruination of my hoard."

Prey squeaked like a boy of ten.

"What would you think is fair?"

The Web Speaks

D.B. Smyth

Everyone out!"

Eckar didn't need to shout for the room to hear the menace in his voice. Council members and guards alike, including Vyx's personal Keepers, fled the Great Hall.

Vyx had been talking to Eckar for *moons* about the premonitions in her dreams, and for moons, he'd placated and ignored her. Granted, she'd only been queen for six moons, but she was *Amma*. He should have listened. Now the dreams had turned to nightmares, and in desperation, she'd called together the Arach Clutter—the governing council of her people's chief village—in hopes *they* would hear her and respond.

At least I know where their loyalties lie, she thought as she watched them all go.

All except Zarah, Vyx's Sister-Warrior from life before the Blessing. She stood at the door while others shuffled past her. Her eyes and the slight lift of an eyebrow asked, *Do you want me to leave?*

Vyx gave a slight nod, releasing her Chief Keeper. Let Eckar think he controlled everyone. It could be useful to her later.

The last one out, Zarah closed the door as Vyx refocused her attention on the man fuming before her. She'd expected more of Eckar. Hellfire, she'd trained under him! But instead of listening to her, he sat at the table opposite the throne, eyes dark and hands clenched into fists.

"Something must be done, Eckar. The web speaks, and you must—"

"Enough!" He punctuated the word with a fist against the table, his chair scraping across the wood floor as he stood.

Vyx was on her feet like lightning. Though she was compact, every muscle and movement of her body screamed danger, a side effect of her years as Warrior, fighting, training, and killing. Most spoke of her—*had spoken* of her—as death incarnate, known only as Poison where her infamy had preceded her name.

Until the Blessing, when the gods marked her as the next mother, spiritual leader, and ruler of her tribe. Her fingertips brushed the red hourglass burned into the flesh of her abdomen by god-magic.

What were they thinking?

"I. Am. The Amma," she said out loud. "Ruler of this land *and* her people."

"And *I* am the SuRaya," Eckar spat back. "Chief Warrior and commander of all the Arachnian armies. Your rule ends where the Wild begins. That is the way of our people." He stabbed a finger toward her. "Wo leads, guides, and nurtures. *Ma* hunts. *Ma* defends! And I *will not* have you meddling with *my* armies or dictating *our* missions just because you resent the Blessing that made you Wo. Do you understand me?"

She hated how he used truth to twist everything else into lies. She *did* resent the Blessing. Resented how it had taken everything she was—fierce, strong, independent, feared—and replaced it with fences, rules, and expectations that she be soft, tender, compassionate. Her sharp nails bit into her palms.

"The web—"

"Enough of this web! No other Amma has ever spoken of it, let alone used it to interfere with the Warriors—with *Ma*."

He was right. Not even the Priestesses, who had been raised to be the next Amma, knew much of the web, and what they did know was not to be shared outside their circle. To speak of it to the Clutter was blasphemous, but Vyx couldn't see any other way.

Eckar stepped around the table and moved to the middle of the room. "And no Amma *ever* has threatened the very foundations of this society by overstepping her bounds because of silly dreams and nonsense. Know your place."

Vyx's eyes narrowed. "You would listen if I were still Warrior."

"But you're not. As you rightly made plain, you are Amma." He sneered, his tone twisting her title into something small and unworthy. This was the *real* Eckar, not the face of devotion and protection he showed when others were present.

"Be careful, Eckar. It sounds like you don't respect your queen."

"On the contrary,"—he crept forward, his lips curled up in a nasty smile—"I live to protect your place on this dais. To keep you safe, secure, free from the worries of the Wild. You are the Heart of our people, and *I* am their Strength. You are now Wo, but I am still Ma. Everyone chooses their path; we all must see our chosen paths through to the end, or else there would be chaos."

"I chose Warrior."

Eckar shrugged. "Looks like the gods decided you were wrong."

Vyx's lips tightened and her fists clenched as Eckar turned and strode toward the door. He paused before opening it.

"And, Amma, try to undermine me again by bringing these dreams of yours to the Clutter or the rest of the village, and I will have you tried for and convicted of heresy. The Heart *must* be healthy for the body to live. Though few, we have lost Ammas who deviated from their paths." He turned and smiled again. "But we've never lost a SuRaya."

Allsphdle . . . shhshg . . . tah . . . shh . . . hasshing

Shhsg . . . shhsham . . . asptah . . . shee

Hasshg . . . tam . . . atish . . . shhg . . . shhhsshss

Whispers raced in waves along a vibrating silver thread, a tumble of soft sounds beckoning Vyx to follow. All else was black.

It was always black: just her, the web, and the whispers floating in the darkness.

She'd discerned early on that the threads closest to the center of the web represented the people of her village, allowing her to identify and defuse conflicts in the waking world before they became problems.

But this line? It ran off into the darkness, past the loops representing the people within her village, Arach. But to where? For three moons, she had heard the call, but no matter how long she followed it each night, she only ever found more darkness.

No. She sent the thought out into the abyss. *I always follow, and I never see.*

The web speaks. You must listen, one whisper replied.

No, she thought again. Her body shifted instinctively into a fighting crouch, a dagger appearing in her hand. *They already call me a fool.*

The web speaks. You must listen.

"No!"

She screamed it aloud this time. Defiant. Angry. No wonder Eckar had dismissed her. All she had to offer were premonitions of danger, without details or answers, and Warriors couldn't be sent to roam the deep Wild without direction. How many moons would it take to send messengers to every village within Arachnia's borders? How many more to get a reply? Whatever the answer, Vyx had the feeling it would be too long.

The web speaks. You must—

"Enough! You've got the wrong girl. I am Ma. I *chose* Ma. How can I be Wo?" Her doubt snuck out in the last few words, rendering them a whisper.

Vyx shook her head. She had turned to abandon the web when a single word broke from the unintelligible susurration.

"Ammaaaa!"

Urgent. Desperate.

It gripped her heart, almost making her fall. There was no room to think. No room to question. Only the insatiable need to protect the one who had cried her name. She turned back.

"I hear you!" Vyx shouted. "I hear you, and I'm coming!"

Faster.

Faster.

Faster.

She raced along the vibrating line, driven by an instinct more primal than her own survival, until the thread blurred—the *darkness* blurred.

Whispers filled her, one layering upon the next in a crescendo of Warrior battle cries and the screams of the slaughtered.

Vyx stopped, her gaze darting everywhere. "Give me something, *anything!*"

"Amma," the voice said again—soft, labored, the sound of death. "Wait. Wait!"

Vyx stepped toward the voice, and in that one step, the dream changed from black to a forest lit by the full moon. It was both devoid of anyone but her and filled with the screams of the dying.

Vyx caught a glint of the thread beneath the undergrowth and followed it forward. The forest floor streaked beneath her feet, as if every step were really ten, until she came to a village and fell to her knees, clutching her heart.

Bodies were strung like festival lanterns at the entrance of the village and crisscrossed the road as far as the eye could see. She had seen death, but this was different. This wasn't battle. It was slaughter.

One of the children hanging from the front gate opened her eyes. "Amma," she said. "Help . . . me . . ."

Vyx shot up in bed, the light of the half moon still shining through her window. *We still have time.*

"Zarah. Zarah!"

Her Chief Keeper rushed into the bedroom, accustomed to the cries that often came in the middle of the night. The rest of the Keepers had grown used to them too, and none but Zarah came to check on the Amma anymore.

Vyx wiped furiously at her eyes, both excited and terrified by what she had seen. "I know where, Z. I *know where.*"

Her Keeper sat beside her on the bed. "Then why the tears?"

Vyx closed her eyes as she pictured the little girl on the front gate of the village. She looked back at Zarah, allowing rage to fill her instead of fear.

"Because I also know what. And I know he won't believe me."

"Then?" Zarah's voice contained no trace of emotion.

Vyx gazed upon the half-lit moon. She knew Eckar would use this to convince the Clutter she was unfit to rule, pushing for her immediate removal *without* the consent of their sister-villages. She also knew that somewhere beyond the Wild that separated their villages, her people needed her.

"Get the others. We leave tonight."

It had been almost five full days since they left Arach, and not one of her Sister-Warriors had asked her a single question. Not where they were going, what they were doing, or why they hadn't asked more Warriors to come along. That's what she loved about them. They trusted each other, no questions asked.

She would have invited them to be her Keepers except she knew that walking her around the chief village wasn't what they had been born for. They needed the Wild as much as the chaos of the Wild needed them.

Zarah was the only one who had joined her Keepers, and Vyx had promoted her to Chief Keeper without hesitation. They'd always followed each other into battle, and as Zarah had said, this was no different.

Vyx glanced at her sturdy Chief Keeper and smiled so widely, the tips of her fangs showed. "You're the best."

"You need to hunt," Zarah replied without removing her gaze from the forest around them. "That smile makes you look crazy."

"We have one more day before we reach Tarantul," Vyx said to the group, her grin even wider. "Let's camp. I want us rested to face whatever awaits us."

The small band of women nodded and set about finding a secure location to make camp for the night.

Once decided, Vyx grabbed her daggers. "Supper is on me." She laughed, the sound a little too maniacal for her own taste. Maybe Zarah was right: she needed the Hunt. Six moons was too long to go without feeling the breath and rhythm of the Wild. The trees hummed, the animals sung, and her entire body felt alive in Mother Creator—goddess of death, goddess of life, goddess of all.

How was she supposed to give this up to be the ruler Eckar and the others wanted her to be? She could be soft, she'd realized since she'd become Amma. Tender when needed. Nurturing and kind. She *was* the Heart Eckar had talked about. Even now, she felt the life force of her people: men and women, adults and sucklings, Wo and Ma. She'd felt every single person, individually and collectively, since the night of the Blessing.

Only an Amma could feel this, and only one queen at a time. It was a gift from the gods, transferred from one Amma to the next only upon death.

Vyx traced the sacred hourglass upon her abdomen. The Shamans had known she was the next Amma as soon as the gods had given it to her. Everyone had.

But I don't want to be *Amma. I am Warrior. I am of the Hunt.* She knew, as her Sister-Warriors did, that theirs wasn't a title but a way of being— as much a part of them as their consciousness or soul. *Why must I give up my ferocity to serve my people?*

She listened for the gods to respond as she tracked some prey.

Snap.

The small noise brought Vyx to a hard stop, her head cocking to the side as she listened. Another snap sounded in the distance, and the Hunt blazed within her, drowning out the call of the Heart as she crept forward in silence.

Until she found *him* creeping through the dense undergrowth in the darkening twilight.

A Cket. In *her* territory. She would taste blood tonight.

Vyx circled out in front of the man, crouching low, and threw herself at him, feet first. Her kick landed, and the Cket stumbled backward, though he was quick to recover. They grappled, each trying to use their body and position to conquer the other. His height gave him great leverage, but her compact, muscled body gave her more power. When he moved to knock her down, she sidestepped and used her weight to slam him up against an old, decaying border wall.

They both breathed heavily. With her forearm pressed against his chest and a dagger at his abdomen, Vyx allowed herself to take him in. He had legs that went for miles, a trait she appreciated in the opposite sex, and his hard, lean body and long frame made her want to wrap her own legs around everything he had to offer.

Shit. She was worse off than even Zarah had imagined if she wanted to *bed* the enemy instead of killing him.

Focus, Vyx.

She leaned in close, smelling the wooded scent of his body. He trembled beneath her hold, eyes wide, and her body shivered in response. She loved this part: feeling the fear of her enemies right before she killed them, listening to them scream and plead until she stole their last breath.

Yet this one was different. His fear leaned more toward excitement than terror. His gaze raked up and down her body, lingering on her muscled arms and legs, and he made no effort to hide his appreciation for her glistening body, all curves and dangerous promises.

"Do you want to die?" Her sharp fangs glinted in the moonlight as she smiled wickedly.

He smiled back, slowly reaching for her exposed abdomen. "I'm sure we can figure out a more . . . interesting . . . option."

"Oh, definitely." She shifted her weight, throwing him hard toward the ground as she brought her knee up to meet his nose. Blood gushed, and his eyes rolled back in his head. "I'm sure my sisters will want to play."

Vyx and her tiny band of assassins crept silently through Tarantul. The Cket had been very forthcoming once Syder took a turn with her blades. She'd always been the most persuasive of the group.

He was a deserter, sickened by the slaughter. He had only been angry enough to leave, though, not angry enough to stop it or alert anyone. So she'd left him tied to a tree to bleed out or get eaten, whichever came first. Either way gave him plenty of time to consider what he'd done.

The roadways were as she'd seen them in her dream: strung with bodies of the dead. She'd take care of them soon, but first she had a group of enemy soldiers to kill. According to the one she'd captured, the plan was to leave a small force behind to deal with anyone who wandered into the city. Tarantul wasn't necessary to hold, only to keep word from spreading to the sister-villages while the Cket army ravaged the land and her people.

And if a force *did* come, they were to burn the city to the ground. The smoke would make an effective warning to the Cket generals.

The Arachnian Warriors were fierce, but Tarantul was a devastating witness to the fact that even they could fall if caught unaware.

Eckar needed to know. And he needed to act, though Vyx still doubted he would.

Tarantul first. Then I'll deal with Eckar.

She looked to her Sister-Warriors and nodded.

The Cket force never saw what killed them.

Eckar glared at the pile of arms Vyx dumped before him. She'd chosen to skip a formal meeting in the Great Hall and instead meet him out on the training grounds. More eyes meant more impact.

Finally, he sneered. "Does the Amma feel better now that she's had a chance to play Warrior again?"

The men and women around them shifted, and low mumbles raced through the crowd. Syder tensed, shifting her weight forward as she reached for her blades, but at a gentle touch to her wrist from Vyx, she relaxed back into her stance beside the female ruler.

"Do you see the markings, Eckar?" Vyx asked.

"And?"

"Who do they belong to?" She needed his voice to carry the news to the Warriors in the back. Let *him* acknowledge the evidence.

"Is six moons so long that the Amma no longer recognizes the markings of an enemy?"

A few in the crowd laughed.

"Is a fortnight so long that the SuRaya has forgotten how to show respect to his Amma?"

Nods and grunts of agreement rippled through the people around them.

Eckar's sneer shifted to a slight frown. He paused and then bowed slightly, smiling. "Please accept my apology if I offended you, Amma. It is simply Warrior banter, and I forget myself while on the training ground."

Vyx ignored the way he used the word *Warrior* as a wedge between her and her former peers. Her Sister-Warriors stood by her; she had to trust that others would too.

"The markings, SuRaya?"

He glared. "Cket."

Curses sounded from the growing group of Warriors. Vyx noticed that most of the Clutter had arrived and made their way to the front.

Thank you, Zarah.

"And by your great wisdom and experience, how old are the wounds?" Vyx knew he wouldn't lie here. Others would soon see the arms with their Cket tattoos. If he stretched the truth, he'd be calling into question his own prowess.

"What is the point of all this, *my* Amma? Is this a field test from the new ruler?" He laughed, and a few laughed with him.

Most, though, held questions in their eyes, and from the back of the crowd came the call, "How long?"

Eckar scowled. "The wounds look fresh. Maybe half a fortnight."

More questions and shouts rang from the Warriors.

"What?"

"How?"

"Where?"

Like Vyx and Eckar, they knew that Arach was held deep in the center of Arachnia, which meant it should have taken at least a three-moon march to collect this many Cket arms at once. The Hunt began rising in the Warriors around her. Vyx could feel it: the chaos, the heightened aggression of Ma, the need to kill.

How long have the Ckets been here? she wondered. *How many more villages will we find strung with bodies?*

Eckar stepped toward Vyx, gripping her arm. "It seems the Amma and I should take this to the Arach Clutter at the Great Hall."

Both Zarah, who'd joined them sometime during the chaos, and Syder stepped between him and Vyx. "I wouldn't do that," Zarah said. Only she could make calm and steady sound like a threat.

Eckar looked at both of them and let Vyx go.

"My Sister-Warriors and I took out a small band of Ckets five days from here."

Cheers and anger erupted simultaneously. Vyx could feel the tension tightening with every revelation.

Heart or Hunt? Do I nurture in this moment or take them past breaking?

"But Arachnia didn't go unscathed. Warriors, children of Ma, I ask you in this moment to place fist to heart." It was the symbol of mourning among her tribe. "Feel the Mother Creator. Reach deep into the earth beneath, from which life comes and to which life is returned."

Vyx felt through the life force of the crowd as Warriors and others alike connected to the deep magic below them. She waited, allowing them to reach deeper and, in the reaching, to have their tension transformed into a tight drum rather than a taught string. A drum she could work with; a string she would break.

"My Warriors, my children . . . the city of Tarantul is no more."

As she expected, the Hunt screamed for blood. But instead of breaking them into frenzy, it rose from their depths as thunder—as a unified battle cry, ready for war.

Eckar looked at the crowd and then at Vyx. "How dare you! *How dare you* put the Amma in danger to resolve our petty dispute!"

Hundreds of hearts that had moved with Vyx missed their beat as the blood rage turned on her. "Who hurt the Amma? We will kill the one who hurt the Amma!" The words spread like wildfire.

"Vyx," Eckar breathed. "Vyx tried to hurt the Amma. You defile this title. Your shame is like a plague, killing Amma's beauty and power. You are meant to heal our people, help our people. You are our Heart. How could you?"

Tears streamed down his cheeks. "You are too sacred to be defiled by bloodshed. Too important to put yourself in such danger. What if you had been killed? Or captured by the Ckets? *Defiled* by the Ckets?"

Gasps sounded throughout the crowd. Eyes turned to her in horror.

"Why have you rejected our protection?" Eckar made a sweeping gesture to the crowd. "Why have you rejected the very Warriors you once fought alongside? *We* are of Ma. *We* are meant to be strong. Right, Warriors? We are the Strength of Arachnia."

"Yes."

"Her power."

"*Yes.*"

"Her safety."

"Yes!"

"We are her might!"

"*Yes!*"

There it was. The frenzy of the Hunt. The string. Vyx could feel it threatening to break. And it wouldn't be in her favor.

"Yet this woman disowns us. She abandons us as she has abandoned her role as the Amma. She is a mother who doesn't care for her young—who believes Wo is less than Ma."

"*I* have abandoned the Amma?" Vyx shook with rage. "*I* have shamed this role?"

Eckar ignored her as he continued to feed the roiling Hunt. "I have protected the Amma for more than two hundred moons, and *never* have we been denied our right to protect. To keep safe."

He pointed at Vyx. "She defiles the Amma. She rejects the gods. There is only one way to pass the Blessing: She. Must. Die."

From Shamans and council members to Warriors and citizens, the training grounds erupted in turmoil. Some fought to protect; others, to kill. Zarah grabbed Vyx's arm and tried to pull her from the area, but Vyx pushed her away.

If I go, I have lost not only them but all Arachnia.

From deep within, she heard the words calling to her: *The web speaks. You must listen.*

"Protect me," she said to her Sister-Warriors, and she dived within, reaching for the web.

Down.

Down.

Down.

She dived until she felt the threads that existed inside her, guiding her to help her people. They were chaos, all vibrating in anger, rage, doubt, and fear.

Standing at the great center, she knew she wasn't enough to calm the web. Not on her own. So she grasped her web and dived deeper, through herself and into the very earth beneath her feet. Her spirit clawed its way through rock to reach the web deep at the center of Life.

Almost . . .

There . . .

Just as her fingers brushed the Life web, opposition yanked her back. Her fingers dug like talons into the rock around her. She would not be denied.

Hurry, Amma. Hurry. Zarah's whisper.

With fingers bleeding, Vyx pulled against the unseen force holding her web. She advanced one excruciating pull at a time, screaming against the pain, reaching for—

Peace.

Vyx opened her eyes to see the Mother Creator grasping her outstretched hands. Like cool water quenching fire, peace flowed from the Mother Creator to Vyx and on through each thread of the web— calming, soothing, renewing.

Thank you, Mother.

The Mother Creator nodded and smiled. *Thank you, Vyx. The web spoke, and you listened. Always remember they need you—all of you, my child. Wo and Ma. Amma isn't one. Amma is all.*

Yes, Mother Creator. I see, and I will remember.

Then Vyx was back in her body, back in the present, with the world raging around her. Only now she could see the web outside her mind. It connected each person, the animals, the land. All of it was part of the greater whole.

When the web speaks, they must listen.

She made the web speak.

She reached out and, gently touching the threads, allowed the peace she'd found within to flow outside her.

The Warriors stopped fighting. People stopped arguing. All eyes turned to her, wide with awe.

"When the web speaks," she told them, "we *must* listen."

Eckar moved toward her. "You are done speaking for the people."

She grasped his thread of the web and twisted, sending him to the ground without even touching him. He clutched at his chest as she held her fist closed, looking around at her people. Her gaze fell on the Clutter members who had gathered, and they took a small step back.

In this moment, her people didn't need tender Vyx. They needed fierce Poison.

Amma is all.

"For three moons, I have heard the cries in my sleep. For three moons, I have asked the Clutter and the SuRaya to investigate. For *three moons*, I have waited for the Warriors to be called to protect. And what have you given me? Placations. Delays. Denials. And *threats*.

"But I will not be threatened into silence. What mother would not speak for her children? What mother would not stand against a claw-bear to save her child? What mother would turn away from the desperate cry of her son or daughter about to be slain? Wo or Ma, would you not stand to fight the beast that threatened to take the life of your child, even if it meant your own?"

"Hear! Hear!"

"Yes!"

"Why, then, does this man accuse the Amma of defiling her role to protect her children?" Vyx pointed at Eckar, who still clutched his chest with a scowl. "When they scream my name, should I not reach for my knives? Should I not give my life that they might live? Should I not rise as the firedragon, poison in my fangs, to kill every last beast that would seek to drink the blood of my young?" Her gaze roamed the crowd, locking here and there with individual people.

"Be the dragon!" someone called.

"Eckar claims I shake our foundations. That in being Warrior *and* Amma, I defile both. That I make one or the other inferior. I say he misunderstands, for Amma is not one. Amma is all. Amma *is* Ma, and Amma *is* Wo. We are *both*."

"But it goes against our customs."

Vyx turned to the council member who had spoken. "Then perhaps our customs go against the gods."

His eyes widened as his mouth dropped open.

"Dear Clutter, I do not seek to take away what is good, only to add to it. In a time when the Cket army marches on our people, the gods. Marked. *Me*. Warrior, not Priestess. Not to exchange the Hunt for the Heart but to *unite* them."

Vyx walked back to Eckar. "I do not seek to replace you, SuRaya. I only ask that you listen when the web speaks through the Amma."

She released his thread and held out her hand to help him from the ground. He stood on his own, rubbing his chest.

Vyx focused on the crowd. "The Cket army marches on to Myssulena. It is time for the Warriors to fight. Are you with me?"

Cheers erupted from the throng of people. "Save Arachnia. Fight for the Amma."

Vyx turned to the council members. "Will you stand with me?"

"The Clutter stands with the Amma!"

She looked to Eckar. "Will you stand with me?"

His jaw flexed, his lips drawn in a tight line. "I will stand with the Amma."

Vyx bowed her head slightly and turned to walk back toward her Sister-Warriors.

"Watch out!"

The warning came from Zarah, but Vyx had already felt the vibration of the web. She turned, avoiding Eckar's blade, and drove her own dagger up beneath his rib cage to pierce his heart.

As Eckar coughed up blood, Vyx leaned in close. "I *am* Warrior. I *am* Amma. I am *all*."

The web speaks, and I am listening.

Queen of the Underworld

Rachael Denessen

It took twenty minutes, an unwanted cruller, and a flower crown for Sef to realize she was being followed.

Sef had just had the worst bad day, and she'd had some doozies. She had come home from learning her dream job had been outsourced, leaving her unemployed, only to find her tiny corner of the world ringing with fire alarms and the hissing spray of overhead sprinklers.

. . . not up to code, uninhabitable, must vacate immediately . . .

The words of her building's superintendent rang like painful gongs through her head as she entered the park, which didn't help the tension headache brewing at the base of her skull and blurring her vision. She'd lost everything, and she didn't even have anyone to fall back on for support.

The first time the man appeared over her shoulder, she ignored him. Like the other slightly amorphous figures clouding her unfocused vision, he probably wasn't a threat. Or even real. Even the hard pavement beneath her feet didn't feel like reality anymore. She didn't have energy to distinguish between blobby shadows.

The scent of fried dough wafted out from a jacaranda tree tunnel, quieting the gong of intrusive memories. Stomach growling, she sped up—purely for the chance of a doughnut. The black-attired dude might still have been a figment of her imagination, but the doughnuts weren't.

Despite wearing jogging clothes and a fading topknot, Sef was decidedly not a runner. By the time she reached the doughnut cart, she had to brace her hands on her knees, panting, as tendrils of hair clung to her face.

"Cruller?" the cart attendant asked. Sef put up a finger, asking for a second to catch her breath. The attendant, not understanding, bagged the proffered cruller. By the time Sef could speak, the attendant had packaged the cruller in a homespun bag and sealed it with a cute sticker.

Now Sef couldn't refuse. Wordlessly—and trying not to pant, as she had reached the time limit for acceptable public panting—she handed the attendant money from her armband. As she zipped it back up, she caught sight of the shadowy figure yards away. Frowning, she breathlessly thanked the girl for the unwanted cruller.

He's not following me. I'm not interesting enough to follow. She sighed and got back on the path, rubbing her temple. *Damn this dude. Nah. If he comes at me, I'll throw this cruller in his face. He's gonna catch a swift kick to the nuts before I run again.*

Feeling better with a plan, Sef raised her head. Perhaps her spine was a bit straighter. A casual sweep of her head kept her rear view in check. The hit of adrenaline did wonders for sharpening her surroundings to better resemble reality. Yet she still couldn't quite feel the ground beneath her feet or pinch herself hard enough to really feel the pain. She looked at the red pinch mark on her arm and frowned.

By the time she reached the thoroughfare, she'd marked her dark shadow every thirty seconds. Never any closer, sometimes a bit farther back, but always there.

Honestly, terrible job. One out of ten for technique, dude. Do not recommend.

Trying to give this probably-not-an-actual-creeper an out, she stopped at a flower crown cart.

At least one good thing is going to come out of this mangled train wreck of a day.

Sef smiled as she ran her fingers over a peony crown. The soft, lovely hue of pink drew her fingers deeper, and she soaked in the warm vibrancy to dispel the garbage of the day. The longer she touched the petals, the more her indignation melted to her feet. Some of the petals followed, earning a sharp look from the owner. Sef smiled, a pleasant warmth easing across her cheeks. It seemed to disarm the owner's crankiness.

Sef pulled the crown from its dummy head and settled it onto her own. "How much?" she asked, tweaking the fit to suit the flowers.

The cart owner's eyes narrowed, then widened. "Uh . . . it's yours. Yeah. You're good to *go!*" He seemed to be speaking to something over her shoulder.

Sef rolled her eyes, her good vibes fading under the pink halo. "Thanks. I really appreciate it." She waved, eager to go home, and was immediately slapped with the reminder she didn't have one.

From there, she turned down the longer, typically more populated path. Violet-rimmed black spots filtered across her vision, drawing the frown back across her face.

She fussed with the crown as she walked. Adjusting a few stems so they would stop poking her demanded a fair bit of attention, so she didn't realize the path was bereft of people. In fact, she was so intent on distracting herself by preening, the only thing that pulled her out of her flowery reverie was the clearing of a throat behind her.

She spun around. Channeling an unfamiliar judo spirit, she swung her house key like a brass knuckle directly into her stalker's face, screaming, "Stay the hell away, you spooktastic, eldritch boogeyman!"

The key jolted on impact and scraped down the man's cheek as if it were stone, scratching but not puncturing. Stunned, Sef looked at the key as the man howled and grabbed at his face. Instead of blood, a flash of scarlet fire flickered between his fingers. The same flame filled his eyes, which were narrowed more in surprised anger than pain. As he seethed, the air around him shimmered darkly, shadows flexing through the air.

"What the . . . ?" Sef looked from the bloodless key to his only slightly damaged face. His face smoothed once more, but the slice wasn't quite healed. The glowing red line refused to fade.

"I could say the same."

As his rolling, inhuman voice hit her, Sef shuddered. Strange. It wasn't a shiver of fear. It was . . . relief?

"Oh, thank god. I thought you were a rapist. I see now."

And she did; she had finally gone stark-raving mad. It explained quite a lot. She flicked her eyes up the long black lines of the man's figure, noticing they didn't lie quite right against their surroundings. Neither did the white hair, strands of which moved about his head and shoulders despite the stillness around them. Well, as long as she was crazy, she might as well dive in.

"You do?" His lips remained parted, as if whatever he had meant to say completely frayed into ashes in the nonexistent breeze.

"You're either a demon or a hallucination," she explained, fidgeting again with her flower crown. There was one stem . . . ugh. No longer afraid for her life, she could fix it.

"If I were a demon . . ." He gestured for her to finish the sentence.

Sef jabbed a finger up under the edge of her crown, took a pensive beat to consider whether the stem was behaving, and then withdrew the finger. A loose tendril of hair fell over her lips. Thinking, she blew it off with a sharp *pfft*.

"On brand for the year. And my life. Either I'm the wrong person, or you want something. Either way, it's probably better than getting attacked."

Silence.

"So you can get on with it."

"It?"

"The part where you tell me what you want." Sef rocked back on her heels, curious now that she'd surrendered her sanity.

"You're coming with me," he said after a beat, frowning. Sef was disappointed. Didn't her insanity have a better imagination? "To the Underworld. I am Hades," he added as an afterthought.

Sef's eyebrows lifted, her eyes wide in surprise. Well, she hadn't called that part.

"No way! No way, no way, no way!"

His features settled back into that calm, slightly smug facade, as though something about this interaction was finally going the way he expected. His body shifted, the darkness billowing out around him. The flames in his eyes grew as he loomed large, towering over her.

"The inevitab—"

"For real?" Sef bounced slightly, her mouth agape. "Are you serious?"

The looming menace paused. "Uh . . . yes?"

"Oh, thank god! Yes! This has been the *worst*. I don't care; I'm out! Come on! Where are we going? How do we get there? Is it this way? Can we go *now?*"

Sef turned away from Hades and started skipping down the path. Then she stopped.

"Wait, if it's far . . . like . . . do you have snacks? Are we prepared? Do we need to stop for water? Snacks? Snacks are important."

She fixed Hades with a serious stare. His lips parted, but nothing came out. She bit her lip, then remembered the cruller in her hand.

"Here. You can have this. I'll get more before we leave." Sef tossed the doughnut at Hades and resumed her light-footed charge down the path, singing cheerfully about saying goodbye to this miserable existence.

"Wait—I—you're going the wrong way!" Hades called after her. "The Styx is that way!"

They arrived in front of an obsidian palace in the center of a gray, misty landscape.

"Where are we?" Sef asked.

"Asphodel Meadows," Hades answered.

"Ah," Sef replied as if that meant anything. In passing, she noticed a severe lack of color.

Well, you are in the Underworld. Did you expect technicolor?

She had to admit to a bit of relief, though. Her conflation of hell and the Underworld had led her to expect something . . . fierier. She was glad her insanity could pleasantly surprise her.

The next morning, Sef found the closet in her room was full of black gowns. She couldn't fathom walking in them. Instead, she used a black corset over a plain dressing gown. She tied the skirt of the gown off to the side so the black stockings and her black high-top sneakers were unimpeded. Once dressed, she went in search of Hades.

Eventually, an attendant found her and guided her to the Grand Hall. Inside, Hades loitered by a tall paned window, clutching an oddly plain black mug.

"Good morning!" she greeted.

She was shown quickly to a seat at the head of the long table. Four attendants lined the top of the table at a respectful distance as Sef sat first, followed by Hades in the seat beside her. It twisted her head for a moment; she'd never seen a table with two place settings at the head.

She dismissed the thought when she scented the tempting crimson within the black bowl before her. Grabbing a spoon from the napkin beside the bowl, she dug into the juicy seeds. When she lifted a spoonful to her mouth, one of the attendants gasped.

Startled, Sef lowered the spoon. Had she been rude? Had she somehow exposed herself? She looked to the man at her side for an explanation.

Both amusement and disappointment crossed Hades's face. "She worries for you because the seeds are spelled—ensorcelled to keep you here."

Sef set the spoon down but didn't let go. Her eyes went to the attendant, who bowed her head, flushing. Sef blinked, coming back to the matter at hand, and waited for Hades to explain.

"Each seed will tether you to the Underworld for one month of the year," he confessed in a dispassionate monotone.

"And you're telling me this, why?"

His eyes flashed, and he considered her silently. When she realized an answer wasn't coming, she leaned back to give herself room to think. One month each? This felt like a test. She wasn't sure of what, of how to pass or fail, or of anything really. Did he expect her to run screaming? If he did, why was he looking at her as if she were a fascinating museum piece?

Peering into the bowl, she carefully shook the spoon until only six seeds remained. Then she lifted the spoon, stared down the demon, and popped the spoonful into her mouth. Now he had no choice but to let her stay. And if she got Underworld fever, she could leave. But now, no matter what, she always had a home.

The attendant gasped again and wobbled. Hades's brows lifted high into his white hair. Once Sef finished savoring the tart yet decadently sweet fruit, she set her spoon down. Idly, she wondered if it tasted so good because it was magic or because she was starving.

Sef thought back to the doughnuts gone by. "Do you have any non-magic food? Like tacos? I'm actually hungry."

Hades snapped his fingers and stew appeared, replacing the seeds. Sef's stomach growled, and Hades's mouth twitched.

"Okay," Sef said after finishing the meal. "What is this all about?"

"Why have you been brought here?" Hades clarified, and Sef nodded. "You are here to reign as queen of the Underworld."

Sef blinked before releasing the most involuntary guffaw the hall had probably ever seen. It took quite a few moments for her to realize it wasn't a joke.

"Wait, what?"

"You have been chosen to bear the curse of ruling the Underworld," Hades answered, his tone falling into an ethereal, deep timbre.

Sef sat up straight. "You want to give me a management job?"

Hades stilled, his schooled features cracking slightly. "That's . . . an oversimplification. The reality is much more involved."

Sef bit her lip and waved her hand dismissively. "What management job isn't complicated?" Sef had managed enough restaurants, shops, and various corporate departments to know that while populations changed, the hallmarks of management didn't. Sure, it was the Underworld, but how different could it be?

I mean, I've managed retail. At Christmas.

Hades opened his mouth to clarify, but Sef beat him to the punch. "So this whole thing is just a really strange job interview? I'd stay in this palace and manage your people?"

Hades's mouth closed, then opened again. "This is . . . correct, but not complete."

"Okay, then." She offered her hand to the demon. Hades glanced at it as if he'd never seen one before. After a moment, he slid his hand into hers, and she shook it. "I'm in."

"A few things must be made plain." He released her hand. "We have not officially been introduced. I told you my name was Hades. I may not have clarified that I am the god of the Underworld."

Sef's eyes widened momentarily. Then she schooled her features back to neutral. As far as fanciful alternate realities went, her mind was doing a hell of a job giving her back everything she had lost in the most fantastical, albeit twisted, ways.

"Okay, what else?"

"There are tasks to complete for you to become queen."

"Like a trial period?"

A small smile played at the corner of Hades's mouth. The god of the Underworld was almost smiling? She must be crazy. Ha!

"Sure. A trial-by-fire period, if you will."

She nodded as if this made sense. "What does it entail?"

"Conquering several challenges in the districts of the Underworld. Once you have demonstrated your ability to rule, you will become my bride."

Sef's focus snapped, and she pierced him with wide, surprised eyes. "Excuse me, I'll do what now?"

"You will become my wife and queen." Hades's firm tone brooked no argument. This did not stop Sef.

"Yeah, no. I'll be your queen, but I'm not marrying you." She sat back in her chair, resolved.

"That's not . . . that's not how any of this works. I am the god and king of the Underworld. For you to become queen, you and I must wed."

"Listen here, dude. You want me to do all that problem-solving? You want me to fix your districts?"

"Yes." Hades succeeded in hiding most of his desperation, but Sef could see a glimmer of the heavy weight bearing down on the god. He needed help. Badly.

"With the number of souls growing at exponential rates, I have my hands full creating enough space for them, let alone meeting their individual needs. I need someone to help me restore and institute lasting balance. I have seen you through the eyes of the Fates. You bring balance wherever you go. You do so by focusing on situations person by person. You meet each new challenge head-on, and you do not stop until you find a way to solve it."

Lowering his voice, he added, "I need that kind of partner."

Sef paused at the earnestness in his voice but didn't soften. "Then find a way. I'll take care of all that, but I'm not marrying you." She fixed Hades with an unwavering stare. Hades's fiery eyes flickered, seeming to burn with determination and a strange pleasure.

Moments passed. Then:

"All right."

A smile slowly lit Sef's face. "Okay. When do we start?"

Hades rose to his feet. "Now."

Hades led Sef to the side entrance, affording her small exposures to household staff, who dashed up to him in various states of harried disarray to ask what should be done about this or that. He answered them quickly, calculatingly. With each interaction, he let his human facade slip further away.

Beside him, Sef squared her shoulders. She ignored the gathering shadows, the flickers of scarlet flame that flashed intermittently between his fingers. While she had all the appearance of precision focus, her head did cock every now and then, as if to consider the sound of a passing gnat. Hades wondered, not for the first time, what exactly her thought process must be.

They rounded a corner into a courtyard. Before they'd moved more than a couple of steps in, a giant three-headed dog bounded toward them, three tongues lolling from his three mouths. Sef squealed.

Hades recoiled, expecting her to run.

And she did. Directly at the dog.

"Puppy!"

The dog stopped in his tracks as she ran at him, yipping with joy as she made contact. Sef exuberantly wrapped her arms around his leg.

"Good boy!"

She let go, only to scratch every part of him she could reach. She backed up enough for the dog to lower his three heads down to her. "This is *so much better* than Christmas!" She bounced excitedly as she rubbed the bridges of the outer heads' noses while nuzzling the middle one with her entire face.

Pleased with all the attention, the three heads licked her simultaneously. They left a trail of dog slobber . . . everywhere. When Sef broke from the puppy love, the hair on half her head stood perfectly in the air.

When Sef turned to look at Hades over her shoulder, she beamed pure joy.

"What's his name?"

Hades considered the woman before him. He had seen that dog tear souls apart on a whim. Now, all three pairs of eyes were fixed, wide and happy, on her. He shook his head to restart it.

"That is Cerberus."

"My dog now," she declared. "He's coming with us."

Four people who'd trailed after Cerberus visibly blanched. Hades just shrugged.

"This should make for an interesting trip."

As they continued their trek, Hades began explaining current issues in the district. The minute easing of tightness in his chest as he spoke indicated that maybe this partnership idea hadn't been entirely mad.

"There's unrest in Elysia. Dissatisfaction—"

His words were lost in a cacophony as they entered the main square of Elysia. Sef frowned, her entire face twisting in confusion, then anger. In the middle of the square, on a raised dais, a man sat on a gilded throne and sneered at a kneeling woman he was using as a footstool.

"*You* petition for reincarnation? You think you've achieved virtue? The only use you have is as furniture, and I tire of you even as that. Begone."

"Yes, Your Highest Honor." The woman rose to her feet, weeping as another soul came to replace her as his footrest.

"Rhadamanthys!" Hades bellowed, his fury shaking the ground. How had this escaped his notice? Every creature stilled.

Except Sef. She stormed up the steps of the dais. Rhadamanthys stared at her in shock, unable to speak even a word before Sef began tearing him a new one.

"What in hell do you think you're doing?" Her voice boomed across the silence. "That is a person! A soul! Not an inanimate object. How dare you? This stops now; I will not allow this disrespectful behavior."

Hades's building fury banked as he watched Sef. Her jaw clenched, sharpening her features into something quite like loathing. She crossed her arms, spearing Rhadamanthys with a vicious glare.

At that point, Rhadamanthys's shock began to fade. "Who do you think you are, speaking to a demigod judge of the dead?" His roar caused the dais they stood on to tremble. Sef didn't blink. Hades took half a step back and suppressed a smile.

"Judge? Judges are meant to be ruled by fairness, not rule their power over the very people they are meant to serve."

The ridiculed woman stood only feet away, too shocked to retreat. Sef beckoned her closer, only then appearing to realize she held the attention of every creature in the crowd. Her mouth tightened, trying to hide her discomfort.

"What were you seeking from this bully?"

The woman frowned at the last word. "Reincarnation."

"Hades," Sef called, "what are the requirements for reincarnation?"

Surprised eyes flicked toward Hades at the back of the crowd. He could tell by the blanching of features that they'd forgotten he was there. How strange, to feel so . . . unnecessary.

"None. It's every soul's right and eventual course."

The furrows in the faces of the onlookers deepened as they returned to Sef.

"I see," Sef said. "And you, oh mightiest of gatekeepers, decided to change that? How many people have you tormented? What damage have you done to the lives of people here and on Earth?"

"I don't know, nor do I care. Get this loudmouthed dust mote away from me," he barked at a nearby footman. "Send her for punishment in Tartarus, and make sure they demonstrate what happens when you disrespect your betters."

Sef narrowed her eyes and smiled. "Oh, a place of punishment? We'll be going there together. I might not be the one to punish you," she said, a hint of regret in her tone, "but I'll find someone who can."

The people began to whisper as Sef pulled a wincing Rhadamanthys to his feet by his ear. She dragged him down the stairs while the onlookers kept silent vigil. Hades steeled his features with far more effort than was usually required. Often, he was already deadened and numbed to everything around him. But now . . .

This is not how this was supposed to go. I did not plan for any of this. Yet he found himself delighted. Warmth permeated him as he watched Sef make sure Rhadamanthys didn't fall down the steps. She led the judge over.

"Cerberus," she called, scratching the underside of his chins. "Will you carry him?" Cerberus happily dipped one of his heads and opened his wide, foul-smelling maw. "Whoa! We have to get you some doggy toothpaste," Sef said. "Now be careful; no bites. He's not a snack."

Cerberus whined slightly, apparently disappointed. The populace around them sighed collectively, either from relief or similar disappointment.

"Hades?"

He smiled. "Yes, Wrathful One?" He'd lost control of his features in a wave of mirth. Like everything else outside her scope of focus, she ignored this.

"How do souls get from here to their new place on Earth?"

"Rhadamanthys's job was to dispatch the souls from here to their new bodies."

"How? Magic?"

"You could call it that, yes."

"And is Rhadamanthys the only one with this power?"

Hades's eyes flashed, and the air around him crackled. "I am god here."

"Of course. So perhaps instead of a judge to send these souls off, we make a doorway or portal imbued with that power? If they can request reincarnation anytime, it seems to me they should be allowed to choose when they go. I don't see the point of the middleman."

"Excellent idea."

Hades held his hands out over the ground. Sef stared, rapt, as the ground quaked and roots burst forth, demolishing the dais, stairs, and gilded throne. They transformed into brambles, lacing themselves into an intricate doorway. Hades looked once more to Sef, the inspiration for this wild tangle. Then Hades conjured peonies throughout the briar, and Sef's face morphed from wonder to a rueful smile, apparently appreciating the joke.

Sef and Hades let Cerberus lead the way down to Tartarus. Hades explained that souls who required retribution for the mistakes they made in life were sent to Tartarus to be sentenced. When they reached the sentencing chamber, the line of souls wound round like a serpent's nest. Hades frowned, his anger darkening as he began to storm up the line, but Sef held him back.

"Tell me what's wrong."

Hades turned to her, furious. "The sentencing line is long. And slow." Taking a breath, he paused and surveyed the area. "And the souls. They are not usually so . . ."

"Distraught?" Sef offered, taking in the trembling creature to her right. They had many mouths but no eyes.

"Would we be able to communicate?" Sef whispered to Hades, indicating the eyeless creature. Hades nodded.

Sef offered the many-mouthed creature a smile. "Hey, there. What's happening?"

They oriented on her, and one of the mouths replied, "This is the sentencing line."

"Yes, I can see that." She sat down next to them, as they were only two feet tall. "But you seem . . . extra worried. I only want to help."

"Help? You don't know what I've done."

"Okay, what'd you do?"

"I committed the worst sin," they confessed from one mouth while the others twisted into frowns.

Sef folded her arms around her knees, scooting closer. "Oh, dear. What's that?"

"I lied to loved ones with one mouth and told their secrets with another."

Sef exhaled through her nose but couldn't quite hide her surprise from Hades. He met her quick glance impassively.

"And that's . . . the worst you guys have?" she clarified. "Murder doesn't top that?"

They turned their head slightly. "What is murder?"

"Oh! I'm sure what you did was awful, but there are many worse crimes. Is that why you're frightened? You fear the worst punishment?" Sef gently knocked them with her shoulder. One of the mouths formed something possibly related to a smile.

"Yes and no."

"Please explain."

The soul sighed. "Well, it's been three days, and—"

"Three days?" Sef demanded incredulously. The soul nodded. She looked at Hades, whose flaming eyes, sharp features, blacker-than-jet skin, and pin-straight white hair were on full display. He no longer resembled the figure she'd met the day before, and he knew it. He waited for this to startle her. It did not. Instead, her narrowed eyes seemed to focus on his slight frown and the tiny furrow in his brow.

"There's been talk," the soul continued from their leftmost mouth.

The right one pitched in. "Rumors."

"Rumors?"

"Lord Aiakos is changeable. He might give one soul, who has committed the most terrible offense, the most casual punishment. Then for the next, who might only have committed the slightest infractions, he will mete out terrible horrors. A grecanae like me just received the fate of suffering each of their teeth ripped out, only to grow them again for all eternity."

"Yikes. What'd they do?"

"He spent eons pilfering *snamezg* treats."

"Teeth pulling seems excessive for a chronic case of munchies."

"I have heard worse for less."

Sef shared a look with Hades.

"It's true," shared another soul, this one humanoid. "Serial killers get off with mud bathing; bootleggers get flayed over hot coals."

"Is this guy a friend of yours, Rhadamanthys?" asked Sef.

He didn't answer right away, so Cerberus nibbled a little. "Brother!" he yipped.

Sef rolled her eyes. "Naturally." Sef thanked the souls and snuck up toward the front of the line.

"What're you in for?" Aiakos sighed across his expansive mahogany desk. The soul before him confessed, but Aiakos ignored him as he read from a scroll lying haphazardly across the surface of the desk.

"Blah, blah, intent to sell, blah, over the border . . . hmm. Let's say, headfirst in boiling tar, then frozen in liquid ammonia."

"That's messed up," Sef whispered. The anger of her experience with Rhadamanthys returned, fiery and wild across her features. Hades found anticipation brewing within him. He couldn't predict what she would do, and the newness of not knowing was addicting.

A nearby dragoness nodded. "In five eons, I've never seen such hypocrisy and injustice." She buffed her long, spiky nails on her dress. Her serpentine tail twisted and coiled nonchalantly beneath her.

Aiakos dismissed the soul. "That's my cue," the dragoness said, giving Sef a meaningful glance as she swept up to the desk with long undulations of her tail.

Sef watched just long enough for Aiakos to sentence another drug dealer with picking lentils off the floor for five hundred years, send a politician to the Asphodel Meadows, and doom a child soldier to having their bones snapped in random order every fifteen minutes before she acted. She stepped into the central area before the desk. When the dragoness came to collect the most recent soul and see them off to their punishment, Hades caught the hint of a smirk.

"Get back in line, wastrel," Aiakos sneered, crossing something off the scroll in front of him.

"Cerberus," Sef called. His thumping parted the crowd. Aiakos's eyes lifted from his parchment to the massive three-headed dog now behind Sef. Above her head dangled one of Rhadamanthys's legs.

"What're you doing? How dare you! You're going—"

"I think not." Sef looked over to Cerberus's right head, which pressed a wet nose to her forehead. She smiled. "Sic him, boy." Cerberus happily trotted up to Aiakos's desk. Aiakos couldn't fight much against those teeth.

Sef turned to Hades with a smile. "Do you have a recommendation for what to do with these two?"

Hades watched her with an impassive expression, though the flames in his eyes flickered. Finally, he gave a slight inclination of his head. "The pollution in the river Styx needs tending." Sef's eyes glittered as she gave a corresponding nod.

To Sef's right, the next soul in line asked, "Will you be sentencing me?"

"Sure. I'll give it a go. What did you do?"

"Rape."

Everything about Sef darkened. The soul stepped back in fear. With no one paying him any mind, Hades grinned.

"Murder hornets, I think."

The dragoness appeared behind her. "Murder hornets? What kind of monsters are those?"

"Oh, you don't have those here?"

"What? They're a real thing?"

Sef allowed a slight smirk. "Umm, yeah. A gift from 2020."

"I don't know how to respond to that."

"Yeah, we didn't either."

Sef looked around at the long line of souls waiting to see what she would do next. "Okay, this isn't going to work. We need a council to avoid"—Sef gestured vaguely to everything around her—"this." She looked to the dragoness. "Know any good people?"

The dragoness smiled. "A few."

"Good. Bring them tomorrow morning. Until then, there has to be somewhere in this haunted house these people can chill." Sef looked around as though accommodations might appear.

"I know just the place," said the dragoness.

"What's your name?"

"Pione. Yours?"

"Sef." She offered her hand. Pione took it, confused. "See you tomorrow. I have some garbage to throw out."

"A hard job, but someone has to do it. Also, thank you for bringing Hades down here. It's been eons since we've seen him." Pione nodded before turning to the souls.

Eons? Had it really been so long? Had his expansion plans distracted him so much, he hadn't noticed what was happening here? Hades turned his wrathful glare on the brothers he had entrusted to care for his souls. The betrayal crested within him and escaped in a flashover of fire that consumed him for a moment. But no one noticed.

"Line sections one through four, follow . . ." Pione's instructions faded as Sef and Cerberus eased back into the crowd toward Hades. He regained control of himself enough to return his face to impassivity.

"Come on, buddy," Sef said, patting the dog, "let's go clean up some trash." As she rejoined Hades, she told him, "These guys are going to spend the next few eons cleaning the River Styx."

Amusement flickered through Hades. "I like your style." He fell into step beside her. "You will make an excellent queen."

At her coronation, Sef deigned to wear one of the black lace dresses crowding her closet. The long sleeves trailed, matching the train.

However, she paired it with her peony crown. She suspected Hades had spelled it not to wilt; the vibrant petals were still fresh.

Hades waited for her in the Grand Hall, standing before two black thrones. When Sef entered, everyone in the standing-room-only convocation fell silent, staring. She focused on the fiery eyes of the Underworld god. He smiled amusedly as he waited, holding an intricate black filigree crown.

The smile steadied her. And in that smile, she found the courage to believe this was real.

When Sef reached Hades, she turned around to face the crowd. Behind her, Hades raised the crown above her head.

"Heavy is the head that bears the crown. Do you, Persephone Kore, accept this duty, to serve the souls of the Underworld?"

"I do," she vowed. Hades lowered the crown to sit among the already-present flowers.

"All hail Queen Persephone!" Hades proclaimed.

"All hail the Queen of the Underworld!" the crowd called back.

The Gift

Jaumarro "Joy" Cuffee

My dearest granddaughter." Shree guided Chara away from the path to a small clearing in the forest. "I've seen many kinds of energy across different worlds, but this is the gift of the Hakura. It is passed from one Hakura to the next when her time ends. When I die, you will receive my gift to heal and to help but never to harm. Take my hand."

Shree's hands glowed softly with lines and swirls. Chara took hold of one hand, noticing how thin it had grown. Yet Shree's hand still felt warm—not the heat of their cooking fire, but the warmth of calming *daryi* tea when it began to lose its burning heat. This warmth seeped into Chara from her grandmother's hand and rolled through her blood, soothing, almost intoxicating.

Shree placed her other hand on a nearby tree. "Now, Chara, close your eyes and focus. Tell me what you see."

Chara pinched her eyes closed and giggled. "I see you staring at me." Even with her eyes shut, she could see her grandmother was not amused. "Oh! There's an old bird's nest on one of the tree's upper branches. It's too light to have anything in it."

"Very good. Go on."

"Spots where arms once were—I mean, branches—but not recently. They feel crusted over. And . . ."

Chara grimaced and tried to withdraw from her grandmother's grasp.

"Not yet. Relax."

"There are tiny bits of hollow grass. So dry. It shouldn't be so dry. The ants are carving it up. So many of them, but the tree doesn't feel it. It's dying." Chara opened her eyes as the tears filled them. "But it's not all dead. Can you fix it, like you did the baby with the fever?"

"Sorry, dear one. The tree's flesh is not like our own. But I can fix this." Shree cupped her hands around her granddaughter's face.

Again, the soothing warmth. Chara saw trees so tall, their branches dipped into a silver sky. They were nothing like the trees that covered the mountain where Chara and her grandmother lived. Their trunks were still wet with rain and smelled of earth and sky and life.

When Shree removed her hands, Chara opened her eyes. "How can I remember that? I could barely walk when we came here."

"I remember it. I offered it to soothe your sadness."

"Will we ever go back?"

"It is not safe. You must stay here so you are not stolen like the others or destroyed like my final sister."

"But you said our Hakura rest in the lake."

The crunch of leaves drew Chara's attention.

"Karou!"

A tall young man approached them. His hazel eyes focused on Chara as he dislodged green leaves from his wavy dark locks.

"I stopped by the cabin, but you were gone. I nearly missed you over here."

Chara tucked a stray curl behind her ear.

"Grandmother was just showing me—"

"Tiny things that carve up dead trees," Shree interrupted with a stern glance at Chara. "We were on our way to market and stopped to rest. It is good you've joined us; the basket will be heavy when we return."

Karou picked up their basket. The three returned to the path and headed to town.

There, Chara made the weekly rounds: healer, soap, vegetable, fruit, oil, cloth, and meat. Every merchant traded for or stocked leaves, herbs, roots, bulbs, and various preparations from their garden.

Wearied from the walk, Shree waited with the healer until Chara and Karou returned for her. Together, they trekked back up the mountain beneath the darkening green sky. Arm in arm, Chara and her grandmother followed Karou, who carried the market bounty.

"You will eat with us," Chara said, keeping her eyes on the path.

Karou always accepted. He helped with the fire, preparation, and cleanup. Afterward, he sat outside with Chara and told her stories of hunting and riding when he was younger.

"Will you ever go back to that life?" Chara asked.

"I don't know if I can."

As Karou looked away from Chara, she could see his tear-filled eyes reflected in the cabin window. She lifted a hand to comfort him, but before she could touch him, she noticed a faint glow around her hand.

Frantic, Chara rushed into the cabin. Seeing her grandmother on the floor, she crouched down next to her. The transfer had begun. Chara tried to place her barely glowing hand atop her grandmother's chest.

"No," Shree rasped out firmly. "It is my time. I will rest in the garden. You will always know I am here, close to you. Stay here."

"But you should rest in the lake with your sisters."

Sadness filled Shree's dull, gray eyes. "I am too weak to make the journey, and you are not yet strong enough."

Chara shook her head. "You told me the Hakura were always healers and, long ago, we were travelers. I was born there. If I try hard enough—if I focus—I should be able to take us back."

Chara closed her eyes and leaned in close to her grandmother.

Chara opened her eyes beneath tall trees that stirred the sky. The journey had taken its toll on her, and she stood wearily. Driven by love and determination, she helped her grandmother to her feet before turning her head to look over her shoulder. She heard nothing. She saw nothing. But she felt . . . something.

"We are not alone," Shree said, "but he cannot protect you here. You are not safe here."

"I can feel it, but I am not afraid," Chara said, keeping a brave face. "Let us move on."

Shree nodded and led the way.

The sky was nearly black by the time they arrived at the lake's edge. Shree continued onto the water in her sluggish gait. With each step, she faded, until she had descended upon the surface in a haze that settled into the water.

Chara tried to follow, but she stood firmly atop the water. The swirls and lines on her hands glowed. Beneath her, she felt a vestige of the Hakura who had come before her. Whispers filled her head. Dizziness. She could not sort them out, and she fought to block them.

Then Shree's voice drowned out all the others. *"Go back."* Chara stumbled back to shore.

She still wasn't alone. Whoever, or whatever, had met them when they arrived was still with her. He wasn't close enough for her to understand, but he also wasn't so far away that she couldn't feel his presence. Shree had said he couldn't protect her, so Chara rationalized he meant her no harm.

Too weak for the return journey, Chara rested beneath a nearby tree.

Chara woke to the ground rumbling beneath her with what sounded like thunder. Opening her eyes and throwing up a hand to shield them from the morning's gray light, she made out the silhouette of horsemen surrounding her.

Casting her gaze to the ground, Chara focused on containing her gift and appearing vulnerable. As she did, the faint lick of water at the lake's shore drew her attention. The surface rippled. Before she could consider retreating to the lake, the riders urged their mounts between her and the water, driving her back toward the trees.

Once they were farther away from the water's edge, one rider dismounted and approached Chara, examining her hands. He traced his thumb several times over the swirls and lines etched into her skin, but she gave no sign of the gift her grandmother had passed on to her.

"You will come with us."

With no other warning, the rider hoisted Chara onto his large, dark horse. He signaled for two other horsemen to join him and for the rest to continue on their way.

Chara had an idea where they were taking her. Shree had told her stories of the Hakura as healers in this land ruled by the Makir. Each generation, the Makir would protect the Hakura from those who tried to steal them away to foreign lands.

But the Makir who reigned during the time of Chara's mother and grandmother had endeavored to expand his kingdom. He left too few soldiers to protect the Hakura, who were divided between the mountain region and the lands surrounding the lake. Many, including Chara's mother, were stolen away during that time.

Whenever Shree had spoken of Chara's mother, she had never been able to hide the emptiness and pain she felt at losing her only child. It was rumored that the stolen Hakura suffered torture and death. Stolen Hakura who had the gift were used to the point of dissipation, when their very flesh was reduced to spirit—a faint mist that retained a mere essence of their gift.

Shree had once recounted to Chara how the Makir had used her last sister in such a way. Shree had seen the Makir's men carry her sister's body to the lake. As her sister dissipated, another spirit—not Hakura—had appeared and made itself known to Shree as her sister joined the others in the lake.

Was that the presence Shree had recognized before she'd gone into the lake, the one who would not come close enough for Chara to understand?

The sky shimmered silver by the time they reached the Makir's castle. Once she was in his presence, he railed against her and her kind with vicious hatred.

"You will restore my son!" he roared through his dense, hoary beard.

"I cannot help him."

Despite his thick frame, the Makir closed what little distance separated them quickly, his hand flying to her throat. His eyes, just above Chara's, did not lower to look into hers.

"First, that evil one from the mountain tortured him." His grip tightened. "Then the other who said she would help did nothing but prolong our pain and perish, leaving us no other to help and no hope."

Chara's mouth opened. Nothing came out.

"Wretched beasts. For too long, this curse from your kind has plagued my house. You are here. You will cure him, or you will die."

He released his grip.

In a crackly, hoarse voice, Chara repeated, "I cannot help him."

The Makir continued ranting. His chest heaved more with every outburst. He flew at her, grasped her shoulders, and shoved his face into hers, pelting her with spittle at every word. She felt his great anger. She felt his overwhelming pain.

But still, she could not help.

Finally emptied of words, the Makir pushed Chara away forcefully, knocking her to the floor.

"Take her away!"

Chara was taken to a cell somewhere below the main level of the castle. For the first time since she'd arrived in this land, she felt completely alone, abandoned by her unseen companion. Cold and hungry, she wondered if she would leave alive or if she, too, would be forced to use her gift to the point of dissipation.

Through a small slit high in the wall, Chara watched the silver sky lose its shimmer and darken. When she heard someone approach, she slid back against the wall farthest from the cell door. There, she closed her eyes and focused on staying calm.

"You must be hungry."

Chara looked up to find a kind face watching her with sad eyes. The woman held a basket of fruit and bread.

"I am Danora, the Makir's wife. My husband called you Hakura, but you must have a name of your own."

Chara stood and stepped toward the woman. "I am Chara, a Hakura of the lake."

Danora shook her head, her eyes never leaving Chara's face. "We haven't seen your kind for fifteen years. We thought you had all perished."

She unlocked the cell and laid the basket before Chara. Then she reached out and gently ran her hand along the side of Chara's face. "But you are real. Somehow, standing here close to you makes me think of my son."

At Danora's touch, Chara felt the same emptiness and pain Shree used to feel when speaking of Chara's mother.

"Tell me what happened to your son," Chara requested as she proceeded to partake of Danora's kind gift. Tucked in among the food, she found a small vessel of water, which she drank from gratefully.

"Fifteen years ago, we were visited by a furious Hakura of the mountain. Many had been stolen, and she was the last of her family. She claimed the Makir should have done more to protect them. With no one left to receive her gift, she said she would use it to make the Makir know her pain and sorrow.

"She was very powerful. No one could stop her from approaching my son. He was a strong young man, but even he could not fend off her assault. A dark cloud formed around them. We heard his tortured cries. Then suddenly, she was gone. He was left there upon the ground, filled with fever and barely breathing. A guard carried him to his chamber.

"The next day, a Hakura of the lake appeared. She had heard about my son's affliction, and she did not want the Hakura to be remembered as vengeful murderers. She claimed she could not cure my son but she could keep him from death until he could be saved."

Chara resisted the urge to comfort Danora. She knew the gesture would betray her gift.

"We were sent out and warned to move away from my son's room before she closed the door. When it finally opened, the Hakura came out looking much older. She waved us back as she staggered toward us, and the air behind her filled with crystals. The walls and floor froze as she passed. When she asked to be taken to the lake, the guards obeyed, and they reported seeing her fade into the water.

"No one has been able to approach my son since that day. The Makir was so distraught, he forbade the use of our son's name until he is with us again."

"But how is he to be saved?" Chara asked as she finished the last of the bread.

"We don't know. My husband sent soldiers to search for any Hakura who remained in the land, but you are the first we have seen. The Hakura of the lake who froze my son was rumored to have a sister, but when the Makir sent for her, she was gone. We are desperate. My husband will test you, and if you don't have the power to save our son, I fear you will freeze to your death."

Danora shivered. Chara's unseen observer had returned and was embracing Danora. This was the closest he had come to Chara, and she touched Danora's arm to better sense him. To her surprise, it was Danora's own son embracing her!

A familiar image started to form in Chara's mind, but she quickly pulled her hand away so as not to reveal her gift.

Too late.

"You lied to the Makir."

"I only just received the gift; I'm not strong in it. If I tried to revive your son, we would both be lost. But he is here. You just felt him."

Tears began rolling down Danora's face, and she clasped Chara's hands. "He is," she whispered. "I just heard him. He . . . he wants me to help you." Danora's chin firmed, and her eyes blazed with determination. "If I can get you out of the castle, can you get to safety?"

"Yes. I will need a horse to move swiftly."

Danora led Chara out of the cell and down the hall. At the end of the hall, she pressed a stone in one corner, revealing a slender opening.

They both slid sideways into a passage barely wide enough for them to fill their lungs. Once they were through, the opening closed.

They edged sideways through darkness until they reached a point where Danora revealed another opening. She took Chara's hand and pulled her free of the passage, where they tumbled into the hay near the edge of the stable. Danora pointed to a dark-brown steed, and Chara knelt briefly, kissing her hand.

"Thank you. I will not forget."

Chara moved quietly behind bales of hay until she was close to the horse. In a blink, she was on its back and charging the stable gate, using the horse's mane for reins.

As the lake entered her view, the rumble of many hooves sounded behind her. The Makir's soldiers were drawing near!

Chara urged her mount over the bank and onto the lake. The horse's hooves splashed upon the water's surface but did not sink into it. At the center of the lake, Chara dismounted and sent the horse back.

As soon as it left her, the whispers returned, and the dizziness. Then Shree.

"Go back."

Chara closed her eyes and focused, thinking of the cabin, the garden, the green sky, and Karou.

Chara opened her eyes to the familiar warm dimness of the cabin where she'd grown up. She crawled toward her bed, but exhaustion pulled at her limbs. Before she could consign herself to sleeping on the floor, hands lifted her onto the bed.

"Karou?" she whispered before falling into a deep slumber.

When Chara finally stirred from sleep, she smelled beef boiling with vegetables and the unmistakable earthy-sweet scent of *daryi* seeds, which Chara knew brought strength. She looked over at the empty bed next to her own and began to feel the weight of losing her grandmother and knowing that, mountain or lake, she was the last of the Hakura.

Karou brought Chara a cup of food and supported her hands as she inhaled the aroma and sipped the broth, allowing bits of meat and vegetable to roll into her mouth. When Karou went to refill the cup, Chara slipped from her bed and sat at the table, grabbing a large spoon. When Karou saw this, he emptied the cup into a bowl and added more. As Chara started in on her second helping, Karou prepared a bowl for himself.

"You should not have gone there," Karou finally said as they ate. "It is not safe."

"I had to take Grandmother to rest with her sisters. It was the only way." Chara looked up from her bowl. "And how would you know whether it was safe?"

"Shree told me many things about your people. You must not go there again. If you do, my—" Karou bit back the angry words and took a deep breath. "If you return, the promise I made to Shree to always look after you will be broken."

They continued their meal in silence. Chara did not wish to argue, but she couldn't swear she would not return to feel the presence of her grandmother and the Hakura who rested in the lake. As she thought about it, the loss of her grandmother pressed down upon her. She would never be able to soothe her grandmother's greatest pain, but maybe one day she could soothe another's.

"Have you ever tried to go home?" she asked.

Karou frowned and drained his bowl. "There is much you don't know. One day, when you are older, I will tell you."

They continued to fill their bowls until the pot was empty. Together, they cleaned up, then walked out under the dark-green sky. That night, there were no stories of riding or hunting.

"With Shree gone, I don't think you should live alone," Karou said softly. "I don't mean—I just want to look after you, if I can."

Chara nodded. "I will take Grandmother's bed. It will make me feel closer to her. You can take my bed, though we'll have to adjust it to fit you." Chara looked up at Karou and chuckled. "We hadn't planned for me to get any taller."

Over the next few weeks, Chara and Karou kept busy. He brought to the cabin only his clothes and the blankets Shree had given him.

They adjusted the bed for his frame. They mended floorboards and fixed the fencing around the garden. Chara taught Karou about the leaves, roots, and seeds of various plants and flowers grown in the garden. And every week, they continued the market run into town to trade the garden's bounty for other necessities.

Chara no longer saw a need to hide the gift from Karou. He had already witnessed her transport Shree home and return. Each day, she took time to use the gift. She felt and understood the trees, plants, and animals close to the cabin. When called upon by the town healer for assistance, she would prepare teas, salves, and tinctures to be consumed by or applied to patients while she used the gift to heal them. At first, it would take multiple visits to get the right mixture, as she couldn't always see clearly what was wrong or how to fix it. Even as she improved and began to heal patients in a single visit, she often doubted herself. If she couldn't heal simple maladies, she would never be strong enough to help Danora.

On what would become their last trip into town, Chara and Karou had finished their trading and were about to head home when they heard a tumult in the street. They pressed through the crowd. Someone was trying to gain control of a horse that had reared up on its hind legs. Looking down, they found a young boy lying motionless on the ground. His life bled out from gashes covering his head and torso.

Once the horse was no longer a threat, onlookers approached the boy. Feeling a tug within her, Chara instinctively moved forward, her hands beginning to glow. As she did, the others backed away, staring at her in fear and wonder.

Chara knelt beside the small figure. Looking him over, she saw both exposed, broken flesh and the cracked bones and severed vessels hidden within. She lifted her hands, directing her energy where it was needed. For some injuries, she had only to gently run a finger over the slight damage. For more severe injuries, she pressed firmly upon the broken flesh until it healed. She continued until every scratch upon the boy's hands, arms, torso, and neck was no more.

Next, she focused on the injury to his head, which had breached his skull. She held his head firmly between her hands until flesh, vessels, and bone were completely knit back together in proper fashion. As she did, she saw the fear he had suffered during the accident. Before reviving him, she offered a gentle memory of her own from a time she had fallen back into a pile of leaves and enjoyed the beautiful sky above.

Lastly, she inhaled. His lungs filled with air, and he opened his eyes, staring up at the sky.

The crowd remained silent as Chara stood and rejoined Karou. They resumed their trek home at a hurried pace.

"I know you've been learning to understand your gift, but how did you know what to do back there?"

"Grandmother once said that learning to use the gift is like the growth of a *masora* vine. Once it has anchored at a new height, it only grows higher. Lately, whenever I go to help someone sick or injured, I'm able to heal them in one try. Maybe this is growing higher."

"He was badly injured. You should be exhausted."

"Actually, I feel like I could do anything." Chara stopped abruptly, her eyes widening. "I-I can do it. We can do it." She turned to Karou. "Come with me."

"Chara, I can't help you."

"If I don't succeed, you can bring me to the lake. I'm young. Maybe they could heal me."

"Or you could perish."

"I have to try. Grandmother was broken when she lost my mother. I was all she had, and I couldn't fix her. I know someone else who is broken in that same way. If I can fix her, maybe I can bring that memory to the lake and help Grandmother rest without that pain. Otherwise, her spirit will never really rest peacefully in the lake. She'll remain broken."

"And if you fail?"

"Then she'll know I tried, and I'll be with her, just as I was here. We'll be together, and she'll at least have the part of my mother that is me. I'm sorry. I have to go."

Chara closed her eyes and focused on the lake, the whispers of the Hakura, and Shree.

"Wait. You need to know—"

When Chara opened her eyes, she stood in the middle of the lake. The whispers offered her memories, feelings, and knowledge. No dizziness. She felt stronger. This time, she spoke to her grandmother.

"Help me."

At her plea, a mist rose from the lake. Hakura who had never passed their gifts on to others added theirs to hers. Dissipated Hakura loaned her the vestiges of their gifts. The sum of these gifts shrouded Chara in a cloud of mist. Overwhelmed by their spirits and emboldened by their generosity, Chara moved boldly across the lake's surface.

As if expecting her, her unseen companion awaited her at the lake's edge. Danora's son, tortured and frozen fifteen years ago, would finally have his chance to live again. Instead of keeping his distance, he pressed close. His presence made her think of Karou. If she succeeded, she would return to him, but for now, she blocked out his face so she could focus.

She proceeded to the castle faster than she had fled it on horseback. The ground scarcely received her weight. As she approached, the Makir and his guards blocked the castle's entrance, swords drawn.

Chara stopped. She had no desire for a hostile exchange. She looked past the men to where Danora stood.

"Danora, it is time for your son to wake and see the sky again." Chara's voice rang with authority as her body glowed within the cloud.

Danora pulled her husband back and waved the soldiers away from the entrance. Moving ahead of Chara, the Makir led the way. When he stopped, he pointed down the hall to the door behind which his son lay frozen. A mist of ice crystals lingered in the hall, suspended in midair.

Chara's whole body glowed brightly as Danora and the guards joined them. She closed her eyes and continued down the hall, protected and guided by the Hakura of the lake. As she approached the door, the mist extended and pushed the door open.

"Don't look. Focus," Shree said.

Chara obeyed. She took up a position next to the lifeless body, pressed her glowing hands to his motionless chest, and leaned her forehead against his. The mist extended to encompass the two of them. Physically, she found nothing broken or damaged. Searching further, she found a cold so deep, the vessel was empty. No living spirit could inhabit such a state. The realization distracted Chara, and her focus faltered. The cold crept into her.

"Don't stop now!" Shree yelled through Chara's own mouth. "Stay with him. He's here. He's right here."

Encouraged, Chara redoubled her efforts, and her whole body took on a blinding brightness. As that brightness seeped into the Makir's son, it first warmed the innermost frozen depths of his existence. Working its way out, it ignited every frozen cell of his body with new life.

Droplets from once-frozen ice crystals drenched both Chara and the cursed young man who remained lifeless upon his bed. Once every cell of his body was restored, Chara opened her mouth, and light streamed from her mouth to his. His chest rose. His lungs filled with air.

Weak and exhausted, Chara lingered precariously above the Makir's son, watching his chest as he breathed deeply.

"Look at me," he whispered.

Chara moved her focus to his face and saw the same hazel eyes she knew from the cabin and forest beneath the green sky.

"Karou?"

Then she collapsed.

The mist that had surrounded Karou and Chara retreated into Chara's lungs, but she wasn't breathing. Shree spoke from her granddaughter's lips once more. "Hurry!"

"Quickly! A horse!" the Makir commanded.

With all the strength and vigor he had once commanded, Karou swept Chara into his arms and ran to the stable, his father close on his heels. At the stable, the Makir helped his son mount with the Hakura who had saved his life.

Karou raced through the wood, holding Chara close. He feared she had given her life for his. At a full gallop, the lake was soon in sight. Without slowing, Karou charged clear of the trees and across the surface of the water. Once in the middle of the lake, he dismounted, Chara in his arms. He laid her body gently atop the water and cradled her head in his lap. Faint wisps of mist rolled from Chara's body and disappeared into the lake.

Karou looked down upon his dear Chara as a tear rolled down his cheek. He had watched her grow up beneath the green sky Shree had found that allowed his disembodied spirit to take form. As Chara's age neared his own, he had convinced Shree to let him befriend her.

A ripple in the lake drew Karou's attention from his sorrow-filled thoughts. Mist rose from the lake, swirled about Chara, and rushed into her lungs. Her chest heaved a few times. She was breathing!

"You did it," Karou whispered as she opened her eyes. He touched her cheek, and she smiled.

"We did it," Chara replied softly.

A faint glow drew Karou's attention to the hand with which he held her cheek. Confused, he listened to the whispers of the Hakura.

Shree's sister had given him her gift, which had kept him from death. Now revived, it would grow within him. The Hakura would live on.

That Which Binds Us

Lex Night

"Shaelynn!"

It was the only warning Shae got before an explosion upended the ground beneath her feet. Heat streaked across her back and would have seared her flesh if not for the dragon blood in her veins.

Chaos surged around her as she struggled to regain her footing. She had come too far to fail now. Defeat here would mean devastation for anyone like her. The soldiers they faced were far better armed than they had expected, but they couldn't fall back.

Shae pushed forward. The Nerati had managed to scatter and ravage her forces, but all her people's sacrifices would be meaningless if she couldn't reach the heart of the fortified base. There, bound in chains, was the last dragon. No one really knew why the Nerati kept the dragon alive, but it was Shae's last hope. For two years, she had planned this day. Her people's liberation hinged on saving the dragon, even if the Elders doubted she could succeed.

The world around her slowed, almost freezing as her boots sank into mud. One more gate. She reached back into her pack for a small bottle of fairy fire that had nearly cost Shae her life to find. It was the one thing that burned hotter than dragon fire, which the last gate had been built to withstand. The Nerati and their science could do little against old magic like this.

The world snapped back into focus as Shae rounded the corner and the last gate came into view.

In an instant, the bottle of fairy fire flew from Shae's hand, arching over the heads of the guards desperately defending their position. There was a flash as fire engulfed the metal building, spreading faster than anything human-made. The sudden light illuminated the terror in the soldiers' faces. Magic like this was supposedly gone from the world, snuffed out long ago by their ancestors. Now, their worst nightmares played out before them.

The first guard was too distracted by the fire to remember Shae was there. She barreled into him, knocking him to the ground with a heavy thud. The others turned to face her, gripping their guns.

They never had a chance to shoot. Shae's second-in-command hurled a bottle of lightning at them, which exploded in a violent spray of electricity.

Emma gave Shae a thumbs-up before Emma returned to pushing back the soldiers who were trying to break through the ranks of mages protecting their small group. Shae wished Emma could stay by her side, but where Shae was going, few could follow.

By then, the fairy fire had eaten through the building's metal and stone, the last barrier between Shae and her goal. The heat as she dashed through the burning wall was worse than anything she'd ever felt before. An amulet around her neck flared to life to protect her from the intense heat, which no amount of diluted dragon blood could have saved her from.

Once inside, the first thing Shae saw was a lift and a staircase. She didn't trust the lift to carry her safely down into the depths below, so she took the stairs. She steeled herself against an attack, though her intelligence had said few soldiers were beyond the last gate. No one was willing to go down into the darkness, except the few scientists who had been studying the dragon for years.

Shae's heart was pounding, and each step brought joy and fear. She had no clue what she would find below, but she had long heard the call. All those with dragon blood could hear the cries of the last of their kind; the roars filled their dreams, calling out to them. She would be the one to finally answer the call.

The stairs seemed to go on endlessly, plunging her deeper into the abyss with nothing but artificial lights to guide her way. The staircase branched off in a few places, but she ignored these openings; her goal was buried much deeper.

She nearly stumbled when the staircase abruptly ended, opening onto a fortified room. Warnings in numerous languages cautioned of the dangers that lay ahead. She reached out, trailing her fingers over the signs. She was getting close.

The room was fairly small, containing just a few desks and computers and, on the far wall, a massive steel door. Shae crept forward slowly, scanning the small security room for any threats. The room appeared empty, but sudden movement caught her eye.

The magic of a spell she had prepared earlier flowed through her as lightning cracked the air, scorching the top of a nearby desk. A terrified man in a Nerati uniform scrambled out from underneath it, crawling away as flames engulfed the wooden top.

"Please don't hurt me!" the man pleaded as Shae approached. His hands shot up in surrender, proving him unarmed.

"Can you open that?" Shae gestured toward the giant metal door standing between her and her goal. The man didn't answer as he tried to crab-walk away from her. "I am only going to ask once more."

She had raised her hands to prepare another spell when he broke.

"Stop! I can't do it! You don't know what they would do to me."

Shae let her hands fall, pinning him with a hard stare. He swallowed nervously, trembling. Was this the first time he'd been this close to magic? Shae might be able to use that to her advantage.

Shae reached into her pack and pulled out another small bottle. "Exactly how thick is that steel door? As thick as the gates above? I wanted to do this the easy way, without having to use more fairy fire, which burns so uncontrollably, but you chose the hard way." She sighed, as if this were all just an inconvenience. "Well, I would start running if I were you. It'll consume everything in this room and then the stairs, and I doubt you're as fireproof as I am." She clutched the bottle, hoping her bluff would pay off.

The man's eyes widened. He may not have seen the destruction she had wrought upstairs, but he knew she had to have gotten through the gate somehow. If he bought her lie that she had more fairy fire, getting through the door down here would be so much easier.

When he hesitated, she lifted her arm as if to hurl the bottle, but his screams stopped her. "I'll do it!" he roared, scrambling to his feet.

His large frame shook as he dashed toward a panel on the wall next to the steel door. It took him three attempts to input the code correctly before he stumbled back.

"I did what you asked. Now please don't hurt me."

Shae held her breath as the door slowly opened. In her anticipation, she nearly forgot about the man, who took the opportunity to bolt toward the stairs. She let him go, unconcerned about him alerting anyone. They would already know exactly where she had gone, and it was only a matter of time before guards arrived. Holding back the urge to run, Shae took one agonizing step after another into the dark cavern.

There, a few hundred feet away and bound in chains, was Azula. Tears filled Shae's eyes as she approached the great beast. How long had its cries filled her dreams? How long had it been down here? Rage replaced her joy and sorrow as she got closer. The scientists who had been studying the dragon had done little to take care of it.

The dragon didn't stir as Shae got close enough to see the state it was in. Its once-great wings were broken and torn. Once full of color, its scales had dimmed to a dingy gray and were missing in places. It looked nothing like the dragons of her mother's stories; it was a broken fragment of its former glory. The pungent scent of dragon blood, a mix of sulfur and copper, filled her lungs, making her shake with rage. The smell brought on a recollection of her mother's teachings, and her heart clenched. She had failed her mother, and now she might fail Azula as well.

Each step brought on a sinking feeling of dread as Shae realized it was too late. Even if she managed to get the dragon out, it would not survive much longer. Once she was close enough to confirm it was still breathing, she realized every breath it took seemed to be a struggle.

Shae was almost close enough to touch the enormous beast, but it hadn't even acknowledged her presence yet. Steeling herself against the clash of emotions surging through her, she reached out and laid her hand on its snout.

Dragons were supposed to burn with an internal fire, but this one was cool to the touch.

"I'm sorry," Shae whispered as tears began falling down her cheeks.

A low grumble startled her, and the dragon finally moved, trying to raise its massive head. The anguished sound it made shattered her heart as a weak voice flitted through her mind.

"You came." The air left Shae's lungs. *"I knew you would. Do not cry, little one."*

"Don't cry? Look what they've done to you!" Shae choked out. "I went to the ends of the world to save you, and it meant nothing."

"It means everything. You have saved me."

Shae shook her head, not understanding. The dragon was dying, and she could do nothing to help it. Maybe if she'd brought a healer with her, but the wounds Azula suffered from were significant. There was no healer alive who could save it. Its great magic would soon fade from the world, more magic lost forever.

"Do you doubt me? Soon you will see." The dragon tried to move once more, trying in vain to get its broken body to cooperate.

"Please, stop. You're only going to hurt yourself more."

Shae summoned what little healing magic she knew, trying to bring the dragon at least a tiny bit of comfort. As her hands moved through the air, the dragon watched silently. The soft green glow from her palms was a waste of magic at this point, but Shae didn't know what else to do. She gently pressed her hands against the dragon's scaled face, tears streaking down her own.

Azula pressed its massive head against her, nearly knocking her over. *"Mortals are such curious creatures. I have lived longer than almost every being in this world, and still you struggle to extend my life. You cannot save me, little one, but I can save you."*

Shae looked up, trying to piece together the dragon's meaning, when the scales beneath her palms began to heat up.

"Never forget what I am about to say: be the magic you want to see in the world, Shaelynn. I cannot be there to help you stop the darkness threatening our way of life, but I can give you this gift. Never let them dampen your flames."

The heat beneath Shae's palms became unbearable all at once. Flames erupted from beneath the dragon's scales, engulfing them both. Terror seized Shae, trapping her in place as the flames danced across her skin. She would die here, consumed by the fire of the last dragon.

Yet even as the knowledge filled her, terror was slowly replaced with tranquility. Shae closed her eyes and leaned into the fire. The reddish orange of the flames wove around her, burning her to the very core. There was pain, but it was so far away, she could barely feel it.

Memories flooded her: the scent of her mother, the cave where she had been born, the feeling of flight. Shae frowned, trying to make sense of the images, but they moved too fast, rushing like the dragon's final flames. She couldn't focus on any single memory as she rode the intense waves of knowledge being poured into her.

The first thought she had that was truly hers was to acknowledge something she hadn't thought possible: Azula had given her the last of its magic.

Once, mortals and dragons had lived together peacefully. Due to their longevity, dragons had been the keepers of history, and on the rare occasions that one passed on, they would let their flames consume them—the final combustion of their magic. The mortals who worshipped them were sometimes granted the magic to be the keepers of their fire.

Those had been Shae's ancestors, the first to carry dragon blood within their veins. Shae knew all the stories, but they had always seemed like fairy tales of a time long past.

The dragon fire finally began to settle into Shae's skin, soaking in and filling her up until she felt like she might burst. She gasped as pain rolled through her body, as her nerves tried to keep up with all the sensory input. She collapsed to her knees and lunged forward, desperate to pull air into her screaming lungs, but all she found was more fire and pain.

Meanwhile, Azula's body was shrinking before her eyes, dissolving into pure magical essence that poured into Shae. She could hear screaming and knew it was her own voice, but the magic had disconnected her from her body.

Shae floated for a while, surrounded by warmth and memories of how the world once was. Magic flowed everywhere, and the skies were filled with dragons. No technology could touch this oasis of magic.

But the memories shifted.

Darkness rolled over her as industry slowly crept across the world, consuming everything in its path. The magic slowly went out of the world, dimming the beauty of everything. This was the darkness Azula spoke of: the Nerati and their weapons. Shae watched in horror as images of the first days of the war flashed through her mind. So many dragons and other magical beings fell so quickly. They had never seen weapons like those the Nerati wielded, monstrosities of metal and combustion. Her siblings all fell.

Agony ripped through Shae with such a profound loss, until she knew she was the last. By the time the Nerati came for her, they had already broken her of the will to fight. For years, she lay alone in the darkness, fearing all magic had been snuffed out, until she began to feel a weak connection. She cried out again and again, but no one ever came.

Not until Shae. Now her body contained the last great magic in the world.

"Protect them," a voice whispered through Shae's mind as the last remnants of Azula faded.

Shae came back to her body after what felt like decades floating through the memories. She gasped in pain as magic pulsed through her, settling into every fiber of her being. She pushed herself up from the damp ground and stared at her hands. She could feel the magic just below the surface of her skin, ready to burst forth.

Extending a shaky hand, Shae released the weak control she had on the energy. Fire burst from her fingertips, lighting up the cave with intense heat. This was no ordinary fire; this was dragon fire.

The last dragon was dead, and Shae was now somehow blessed with its magic. Shae rose slowly, mindful of how the world spun. Oh, how it lived! The entire cave was alive, and she could feel every small creature scurrying across the ground, each a small spot of energy. She could feel the energy ebbing and flowing around her. She stretched her senses out above and felt the others still fighting. She saw bursts of magic here and there as they fought the Nerati to buy her more time.

She swore under her breath. *How long have I been down here?* The others needed her help, and now she had more than enough magic to do so.

A grin spread across Shae's face as she sprinted back to the door. No guards waited for her, so maybe she hadn't been down there as long as she feared.

She hesitated at the base of the stairs, her senses screaming. Reaching out with her new magic, she sensed several Nerati about halfway up the stairs, along with some monstrosity of metal that made her head ache to try to decipher. The machine's iron made it almost impossible for her to make out what it was, but it was most likely a trap.

Shae took a moment to center herself and think. The staircase wasn't an option unless she wanted to fight a small army by herself. The lift was most likely compromised as well. Even with the dragon's magic, that sounded like a great way to get herself killed.

She backed away from the stairs and began pacing across the small room. There had to be another way out. Maybe through the cave? The Nerati had kept Azula in chains, even though the dragon had been too weak to be a threat. Perhaps they'd been afraid that Azula would unleash its magic and break free. Now that the magic was Shae's, it burned through her, aching to be used. If she could use the dragon's flames, maybe she could tap into other powers.

The trip down had been utterly exhausting, but Shae felt revitalized now. Her entire body felt lighter, which gave her an idea. Did dragons fly on wings or magic? There was only one way to find out.

Shae acted purely on instinct and the knowledge now buried deep within her mind. At first, nothing happened. Then all at once, the magic began to spill out of her, taking on an almost tangible appearance to wrap her in golden strands. She laughed gleefully as she slowly floated upward and turned her attention to the stone ceiling above her. Melting stone was nothing for a dragon, but Azula had been badly injured and weakened when the Nerati had brought it there. With the magic running through her, burning herself free seemed a simple task.

For the first time in generations, the world would feel a dragon's powers. The Nerati had trapped Azula so far from the sunlight and open skies, but now its magic would be free once more. The Nerati did not understand what was coming for them.

Shae let her flames surround her, and the intense heat bored through the soil and stone. Magma poured down around her, but she was protected by the golden magic swirling around her. Meanwhile, her mind spun with endless ideas of what she could do with this blessing. She would be able to help her people in so many ways. So few had believed she could make it this far. Could she alone turn the tides of the war?

Shae burst through the ground in a spray of fire and ash, startling a group of Nerati. They scattered, screaming for help as she flew close to them, her flames scorching the ground below. She found the first of her fellow soldiers in the ruins of the front gate, where they must have taken cover once the fairy fire had burned through. She strode confidently toward them, daring any Nerati to challenge her and her newfound powers.

"Shae?" called a shaky voice as she crossed the melted threshold. Emma rose slowly, their mouth opened in shock. "W-what happened to you? You . . . you're burning up!"

Shae lifted a hand to see her magic still swirling around her.

"The dragon gave me a gift, but I couldn't save the dragon. We should go now while the Nerati are withdrawing deeper into the base. This may be our only chance to fall back without more bloodshed."

Her friend shook their head. "But, Shae, we could take the base! Capture some of their soldiers!"

Shae held up a hand. "And how many more would we lose trying to take a useless base? We came here for the dragon, and now I have its powers. I have no idea how they work, so we should collect our wounded and retreat. We dealt them a great blow today. For now, we get out of here and live to fight another day. Fall back."

Emma looked like they might argue but nodded and began to signal the others. Slowly, they carried their wounded and dead back to the portal they had used to launch the surprise attack. Two exhausted mages kept the portal open, but they looked ready to collapse. They had others who could take up the strenuous task, but it was best to move quickly.

Shae watched over the group as they moved through the portal, keeping an eye out for enemy soldiers. Her little show of burning her way out of the cave seemed to have spooked the lot of them.

Shae and her people had lost the last dragon, but they had gained great power. She stared down at her hand, watching as magic danced across her skin. Would this be enough to help them end the war?

"Shaelynn, everyone is through the portal," Emma said, motioning for her to follow them.

Shae had been through hundreds of portals, but never had the magic buzzed through her like it did this time. The two mages staggered back, their eyes wide. Could they feel it as well?

She didn't have time to question them as she was whirled away to the safety of the last great city of magic. A few towns had managed to escape the Nerati's magical purge, but none compared to Ashe Haven. The walled center was protected by ancient magic, which had managed to hold back every attack the Nerati had launched on it so far.

Healers had already started tending to the wounded when Shae arrived, and the room was filled with shouted directions. Shae tallied the numbers of wounded and dead in her head. It was always too many. Every death took another bit of magic out of the world and brought them closer to extinction. She clenched her fists.

"Shae!" Emma whispered urgently.

Shae's head snapped up. Lights throughout the room were flickering. Her magic had risen to the surface with her burst of emotion. Embarrassed, she took a moment to center herself.

"Are you okay?" Emma asked, looking around the room.

Shae gave her friend a brief nod before leaving the room, ignoring the stares of the others. Emma deserved better, but Shae couldn't express to them how she was feeling. Her mission had been both a success and a failure. She held the balance of the world and the lives of every magical being in her hands. How could they understand the responsibility that had been placed on her shoulders?

Shae would need to report to the Elders soon, but there was one place she needed to go first. The halls of the base where the portal anchor was housed were always packed with people. The endless war rarely left a lull, so there was always some form of activity.

Ignoring them all, Shae made her way to the shrine of Mixas. The shrine was housed in a small room at the south end of the base. It was set far away from most of the hustle and bustle. There, kneeling before the goddess, she found her mother.

Her mother's face lit up as she turned to see who had come in. "Shaelynn, my dearest."

Shae couldn't help but grin as she helped her mother stand, pulling her in for a hug. She could count on few things in her life, but where she would find her mother anytime she left was one of them.

"Mixas has blessed me once more." Her mother pressed a soft kiss to Shae's cheek. "Did you find Azula? You must tell me everything."

Shae took a step back from her mother, unsure where to start. "I did, but the dragon . . . didn't make it." Emotions flooded her mother's face. "But I did bring home a gift." She held her palm out, relaxing the shaky hold she had on the magic and bringing life to a small flame. "Azula gifted me its magic."

Her mother looked up at her, tears gathering at the corners of her eyes.

"Shae . . . this is incredible. The day you were born, I said you were a gift from Mixas and that they had a plan for you. No one believed in this mission except you, and now you have brought a dragon's flames back to us." Her mother cupped her face. "You are the magic this world needs."

Shae had held her composure so well until that moment. She let her head fall forward, resting it against her mother's.

"What if I fail? You know the Elders hate anyone with dragon's blood. They think our blood is a curse, and they told me this mission was doomed from the start."

No one had realized how closely magic was tied to beings such as dragons until it was too late. Once they did, the Elders had scrambled to preserve the last remnants of magic in an attempt to stop the Nerati. Yet they had fought Shae every step of the way on her mission to save Azula. No one had believed she could rescue the dragon. Technically, she had failed, and the Elders would use that against her.

"You won't. Mixas is with you, and now so is Azula. You will lead our people to peace, no matter what the Elders say. I only wish I could be there to see it."

Knowing this was the closest her mother would get to seeing the end of this war made Shae's heart ache.

"You should go. I can feel the magic weakening." Had her mother's last ties to this world always been so fragile? Shae hadn't been able to feel the magical energy like she could now. Her mother had used the last of her magic to bind herself to the shrine to watch over Shae after she passed.

Her mother pressed a soft kiss to her forehead. "I am proud of you, Shaelynn. You will bring light and magic back to this world."

It hurt to see her mother fade away, the tiny flicker of her magic returning to the statue of Mixas. She kept vigil whenever Shae fought and only returned once Shae was home safe. One day, her magic would fade, and Shae's last connection to her mother would be gone. She wanted to bring peace to the world before that happened. She wanted her mother to be able to rest in peace.

A soft knock on the doorframe was Shae's only warning before Emma entered the room. "Sorry to interrupt your time with her, but the Elders want to see you." They hesitated for a moment before asking, "What will you tell them?"

"The truth. Azula passed its flame to me, and I plan to use it. For too long, they have doubted the worth of anyone descended from the dragons." Shae glanced back at the goddess, saying a silent prayer to them. "It's time I showed them how wrong they are. We are taking the war to the Nerati."

"You know the Elders will never approve of that, Shae. There is too much history there. The Nerati used our blood to learn how to take the dragons down. The dragons were the best defense we had, and they failed. Why do you think you can succeed in their place?"

Shae contemplated the painful doubt in Emma's words, deciding the best way to respond. The Elders were some of the last mage teachers in the world. They had been chosen to protect the waning magic from the Nerati. Shae was one person standing against their power. One person whom the last dragon had selected.

"The dragons trusted our ancestors with their fire." Shae's voice shook with emotion and resolve. "Their magic still runs in our veins. People like the Elders, who only see the bad and call us cursed, diminish everything the Nerati did to us. The Nerati weaponized our blood against all of us, which was not our fault. Now I have a chance to change the narrative, Emma. The Elders may have great magic of their own, but never have we had an opportunity like this. They want to keep the coming tide at bay, but the Nerati will overwhelm us eventually. We have to push back."

Emma's face crumpled as they reached for Shae and pulled her into a tight hug. She let them give her strength. She would need it to argue against the Elders.

"We do this together, friend. You keep that passion, and everyone here will follow you."

"They will always doubt me and question my resolve, but this isn't for me. It's for all of us. I have to make them see that. We have a war to win, but we can't do that if the Elders refuse to participate. Azula trusted me, and I am not going to let them forget that."

Legend of Ardmire Castle

Sianyn Leigh

Early-morning silence fell heavily over Ardham Forest, cloaking the thick foliage in an oppressive pall. No birdsong brightened the gloomy atmosphere, and no game animals sprinted across the dew-dappled trails. Even Rewan, laden with rider and gear, made barely a sound as he clopped slowly along the path, each hoof fall muffled as if echoing from another world. The eerie quiet unsettled Sir Trevyr, and he shifted in the saddle against the creeping unease slithering into his bones.

Legend claimed Ardham Forest was haunted. Sir Trevyr had seen enough over the years to believe it. Many a hunter had wandered into its depths, never to return. At night, strange lights flickered through the boughs like dancing spirits, and beastly groans emanated from darkened recesses. Some said, if you walked the edge past midnight, souls of the long dead reached out with an icy grip to drag you to the Underworld. Peering into the mists curling around ageless trunks and tangles of grasping vines, Sir Trevyr could well imagine bony fingers clutching at his ankles and cloak.

But the forest held a deeper secret, something much more terrifying than the cold hand of death. At the center of the woods, cracked and crumbling from centuries of neglect, sat Ardmire Castle, lair of Flametongue the Great Wyrm. Sir Trevyr had sworn to vanquish the treacherous dragon, to finally rid the countryside of the malicious blight and bring glory to king and country.

Now that his target sat just beyond the next thicket, Sir Trevyr's resolve fractured, and he tightened his fingers around the reins to ease their trembling. He couldn't turn back, not with the enemy army almost at the border and everyone he'd ever known depending on him. Destroying the dragon wouldn't just bring glory to his name; it would deliver the whole of Kergory. For deep within the lair of Flametongue sat a legendary weapon of such might, no army could dare stand against them. The kingdom's long-lost power would be restored, and the people would be safe and thriving once more. If he didn't come back with the prize, he wouldn't come back at all, and every soul in the kingdom would be doomed.

A hero's welcome was much preferred to a hero's funeral, and Sir Trevyr had come prepared to win. The dozens of knights who had fallen to the great wyrm's wrath had all shared one particular weakness: they had all been flammable.

Sir Trevyr was certainly flammable as well, but he had an edge no one else before him had possessed. For the past year, he had been perfecting a fireproof shield, molding together layers of wood, metal, and leather and coating them over and over with a special mixture of his own design. He had also eschewed the traditional heavy armor in favor of thick leather braies and matching tunic to allow ease of movement and speed.

Combining agility with his specialized shield, he could get close enough to the dragon to lay a fatal blow, he was sure of it. The creature was, after all, merely flesh and blood. All animals, no matter how fierce they seemed, had a soft spot. He just needed to cover his own—*all* his soft, combustible flesh—long enough to find Flametongue's.

Thick trees and old-growth vines ended with such an abruptness, Sir Trevyr gave a startled yank on the reins. Rewan snorted in complaint, pushed at his bit with his tongue, and stomped one impatient hoof. Sir Trevyr patted the horse's neck consolingly, whispering a calming phrase as he looked around the suddenly new surroundings.

Where trees and wild brush should have been, the ground lay

scorched and barren. Ragged remnants of trunks and branches edged the unnatural clearing, reaching for the sky with blackened points. Smaller, more gruesome charred bits lined the faint impression of a path, dotted here and there with arms from the royal blacksmith. Sir Trevyr grimaced and bowed his head toward the remains of his fallen comrades in a silent farewell.

Beyond the haphazard skeletons rose the walls of Ardmire Castle, the stones a muted black from countless blasts of dragon's breath. A blackened gate, twisted from repeated lashings of heat, bowed out from its moorings, the row of spikes at the top creating the silhouette of an angry maw against the lightening sky.

Sir Trevyr swallowed back the fear the mere sight of the menacing castle aroused. He would die here, or he would die in the battle that would soon consume his beloved homeland. It made no difference to him, but it did to his mother and sister and to all whom the kingdom sheltered. He had to give them a fighting chance, even if that meant facing the dreaded beast on his own. He would not falter now.

Sir Trevyr dismounted, unstrapped his sword and shield from the saddle, and gave Rewan one final loving pat. Turning the horse around with a guiding hand on his bridle and a grunted command, the knight watched as the chestnut destrier trotted back the way they had come. He had been a good mount, perhaps even a friend. There was no reason he should suffer the same fate as his poor rider.

Drawing his sword and hefting the sturdy triple-layered shield on one arm, Sir Trevyr took a deep breath and turned to face the gate. Taking a few steps forward, he planted his heels in the center of the burned clearing.

"In the name of King Jovarn, I, Sir Trevyr, vow to vanquish the Wyrm of Ardmire and claim the sacred treasure for the land of Kergory!"

His declaration echoed across the imposing wall, sending a host of sparrows from their perch. He waited, eyes sharp, shoulders tense for any sign of the dreaded dragon. All remained silent except for the flutter of wings and irritated chirps of the disturbed birds. Drawing in another, deeper breath, he called again.

A faint clanging reverberated through the windowpanes overhead, not particularly loud but insistent enough to distract. With a labored sigh, Lena closed the tome she had been studying and marched over to peer into the curving periscope that twisted through the castle with a series of complicated tubes and mirrors, providing a full view of the grounds. Adjusting the focus with the twist of a knob, she slowly rotated the contraption, searching for the source of the disturbance. At the gates, a man stalked in an agitated circle, banging his sword on his shield and hollering about "king and country."

Lena rolled her eyes with a huff. Not another one. Did they never learn? Over and over with these blasted warriors and their proclamations of victory. There was never anything so droll as a conquering knight, of which there seemed to be an endless supply no matter how many she left strewn on the path. She just wanted to be left alone with her research, her mechanics, and her now decidedly tepid tea.

With a shrug, Lena turned to the long control panel set into the wall next to the periscope. A series of levers, knobs, wheels, and pulleys weaved in and out of the panel, each marked with archaic symbols she'd learned at her father's knee. If this newest guest wanted to go out like all the others, it was no nevermind to her. She had more important things to do.

A rumbling and clanking sounded through the castle as she yanked down one of the levers. The combustible system whirred to life with a familiar soft vibration, followed quickly by a startled scream. Lena smiled and glided back to her chair and her book, confident she wouldn't be disturbed anymore for the day.

After his challenge had gone unanswered, Sir Trevyr had resorted to shield thumping and whooping in the hopes of raising the dragon. Perhaps the old beast had grown deaf or, better still, abandoned the crumbling ruins for better climes. Such a stroke of good luck the knight would have been more than happy to accept.

An ominous rumbling soon dashed that idea, and Sir Trevyr ceased his circling as Flametongue the Great Wyrm finally made his appearance.

The dragon's head rose from behind the wall, higher and higher on an impossibly long neck. Dark-gray scales glinted in the morning sun, and eyes burning with the very embers of hell glared at the frozen knight. Large, square jaws, lined with razor-sharp scales and filled with teeth the size of daggers, opened in an angry grimace, and Sir Trevyr's knees nearly melted into pudding.

Flametongue clicked his tongue in annoyance, hissed, and let loose the stream flames for which he'd been named. Sir Trevyr couldn't hold back the strangled scream that burst from him as he crouched and rolled to the side, narrowly escaping the abrupt blast.

The ground smoldered where Sir Trevyr had stood only seconds before. Not daring to contemplate what might have happened had he been even a second too slow, Sir Trevyr shuffled about the edge of the clearing while he scanned the beast for a weak spot. Flametongue followed the knight's movements with a pendulous swing of his giant head, no doubt waiting for him to stand still long enough to unleash another blast. Sir Trevyr didn't plan to give him the opportunity, though he could already feel his feet slowing from the exertion of carrying the heavy shield. He'd have to make his move soon, or he'd lose the advantage.

Sir Trevyr feinted right, and in the moment it took Flametongue to adjust his head and follow, he saw it. There, just below the jawline, was the pale gleam of exposed flesh, where the scales didn't quite overlap. That was where Sir Trevyr had to strike. He just needed to get close enough to drive his sword into that strip and through the dragon's unprotected jugular.

The telltale click-hiss of the dragon's tongue alerted Sir Trevyr to another attack. Throwing his weight forward, he curled into a somersault, rolling to the foot of the wall as another stream of fire erupted overhead. Hunching down behind his shield and raising his arm high enough to protect his head, Sir Trevyr scurried along the wall toward the gate, searching for an opening in the bent bars. The sides of the gate didn't quite meet, creating a gap large enough for a child to slip through, but perhaps too narrow for the grown knight. He might be able to pull them farther apart, but that would require dropping his sword for a few precious moments.

Weighing the risks of temporarily relinquishing his weapon made him pause just long enough for Flametongue to pinpoint him again. Sir Trevyr barely had time to cower under his shield between the chilling click-hiss and the release of the dragon's breath. The layers of material and resilient coating protected him from the fatal flames but not the blistering heat. As the fire passed over the shield and flowed around him, his skin tightened and cracked, and hair singed along his exposed crown. He struggled to draw in suddenly oven-hot air as sweat flowed into his eyes and loosened his grip on the sword hilt. The intense heat radiated through the shield, and Sir Trevyr screamed as the flesh of his arm blistered and peeled under the leather sleeve.

The fire ended as Flametongue ran out of breath and paused to assure himself the knight had been dealt with. Knowing he would not survive another direct attack, Sir Trevyr let his now smoking shield drop to the ground and dove for the gap in the gate. Adrenaline and desperation forced his body through the narrow space, and he sprinted toward the great wyrm crouched just on the other side of the wall.

Twisting the sword in his hand, he lifted his arm up and back, gripping the sword as he would a spear or javelin. When Flametongue reared his head back to take another breath, the knight hurled his weapon with everything he could muster.

Sir Trevyr stumbled and fell to his knees, exhausted and helpless now against the enormous dragon. He watched as the glinting steel sailed through the air and found its mark, impaling Flametongue in his weak spot. The dragon clicked his tongue fruitlessly several times, roaring with the sound of steel on steel. The burning eyes dimmed before winking out entirely. The moans faded away as the jerky, disjointed bobbing of his long neck finally grinded—*grinded*—to a halt.

Sir Trevyr had won. Flametongue the Great Wyrm was dead.

The squeal of unforgiving metal ending in an ominous clank sent Lena racing through the castle corridors for the courtyard. The gears of her beloved guardian had stopped turning, and she feared the worst: that a knight had breached her sacred walls. Since her grandfather's time, Flametongue had stood sentinel over the gates of Ardmire, safeguarding not only Lena's family but the secrets they preserved. After all this time, she couldn't believe a mere soldier had bested her most-prized contraption.

But there in the courtyard stood the unmistakable figure of a knight, gazing curiously up at the suspended dragon with a puzzled squint and a hand rubbing absentmindedly at a blistered patch of scalp. The hilt of his sword jutted out from Flametongue's skull hinge, the blade wedged between gears and joints and into the ignition mechanism of the flamethrower. For the first time in nearly a hundred years, the dragon lay still.

"No!" Lena stomped over the broken tiles of the walkway toward the knight, pleased to see him jump at her sudden appearance. "Look what you've done! Do you have any idea how delicate that mechanism is? No, you just trespass on my property, wreaking damage and havoc however you please. Did it ever occur to you the gates are closed for a reason?"

The startled knight dutifully stepped out of the way as she bore down on him and swept past with an irate wave of her hand to inspect the damage done to her dragon. She brushed the unruly curls away from her eyes as she peered up at the sword, wondering how she could clear the jam without inflicting further harm.

"Excuse me," the knight ventured, interrupting her mumbling. "That's a machine? Brilliant."

Lena whirled on him, pinning him with a deprecating stare. "Of course it's a machine, you ninny. Dragons aren't real." With a huff, she turned back to her task, grumbling, "Not that you blockhead knights ever figured that out."

"So," he started again, "all this time, all the other knights . . . it's been a machine?"

She rolled her eyes. "How did someone as dense as you manage to cause all this?" She gestured to her defunct automaton.

The knight had the decency to look apologetic. "Flame-retardant shield?"

"Gods above, help us! They're getting smarter!" She threw her hands to the sky before leveling a glare at him she hoped burned as bad as the blistering on his head. "Well, don't just stand there gaping at me! Help me get the damned thing out. You broke it; the least you can do is help me fix it."

Confusion still etched in his features, the man bobbed his head and held out his hand to comply. Using the knight's knee as a stepping stool, Lena reached up to grasp the sword hilt. Wiggling it back and forth, she pulled on the blade steadily, hoping to free it without pulling the neck gears with it.

"Let me get this straight," the knight said, his voice muffled against her skirts as he braced her legs. "My fellow knights have been coming here to battle a dragon and retrieve the treasure of Ardmire, only to be killed by this contraption? And you just let it happen?"

The sword pulled free with a jerk, and Lena tilted backward alarmingly, swinging her arms for balance. The edge of the blade skimmed dangerously close to the knight's shoulder. His undignified squeal let her know he was well aware of how close he'd come to being cut by his own weapon.

"Well, you're hardly coming here with good intentions, are you?" Lena snapped as she reclaimed her balance. She hopped from her perch and tossed the sword to the ground in contempt. "Castles have walls for a reason. If you, or any other knight, are looking to breach them, you get what you deserve."

"The intention was to kill a vicious dragon!"

"Then their deaths were self-defense!"

The knight sputtered, obviously unsure how to respond to her logic, and Lena tossed him a triumphant smile. "If you lot had minded your own business, none of your great comrades would be strewn about my walk right now."

She waved her hands at him in the universal gesture of *shoo* and headed back for the castle. She needed her toolbox if she were to have any hope of repairing poor Flametongue.

The knight stumbled over his feet in his rush to follow her.

"Be that as it may, I must inform you I've come here on a great quest and I cannot be deterred now, not by machine and certainly not by . . . by . . . I'm sorry, what are you?"

Lena spun on her heel, facing him with her head held high. "I am Lena, Keeper of Ardmire."

The knight gave a deep bow. "I am Sir Trevyr the Unlikely, at your service."

She smirked at the title. "What an unfortunate name."

His head bobbed reluctantly. "Accurate."

Resuming her march toward the castle, she called over her shoulder, "So, Sir Trevyr the Unlikely, why have you abused my property and my sanity so early on a lovely day?"

"To find the legendary weapon guarded by Flametongue the Great Wyrm and bring it back for the glory of all Kergory." The sentence rolled off his tongue with all the ease of a child reciting his letters. "And it's quite urgent, I might add. The armies of Aesloras have almost crossed our borders, and they are not known for mercy. King Jovarn needs a mighty weapon to turn the tide and save the kingdom."

"A mighty weapon?" Her tone had a mocking lilt she didn't try to hide. "And what would that be? Does the legend say?"

Sir Trevyr followed her across the threshold into the main hall, coming up short as he took in the floor-to-ceiling bookshelves that lined the hall and overflowed with scrolls, tablets, tomes, and all manner of recordkeeping. Tables, benches, and desks littered with half-finished projects, stacks of research, and jumbles of vials and pots squatted at random intervals throughout the room, creating a maze that was part laboratory, part workshop, and part library.

"It's a, uh . . . the Legendary Artifact," he stuttered, twisting his head this way and that.

Lena ran her fingers along the spines of heavy tomes as she walked the length of a shelf, looking for a particular title. With a gasp of triumph, she pulled the leather-bound book from its place.

"And what is it, this artifact?" she goaded, fully enjoying teasing the clueless knight. She flipped through the pages as he fumbled for an answer, landing on a full-spread schematic of Flametongue's inner workings.

"Uh, it's an artifact . . . of legendary properties . . . that . . . strengthens the kingdom and empowers the king?"

He had gained some conviction in the middle of his sentence but seemed to lose it by the end. Lena softened her mocking grin, taking pity on him. It wasn't his fault the rest of the kingdom believed in silly tales and never bothered to discover the truth for themselves. They were never taught to think beyond their safe farms and royal halls.

The kingdom had once thrived with all manner of scientists and inventors, but one mad king's desire for ultimate power had swept them nearly all away in a ravage of fire and persecution. The knowledge stolen from laboratories and libraries was corrupted and weaponized, used to forward the monarchy's despotic ends. Any machine devised for the betterment of society lay disregarded and forgotten, useless to his consolidation of power, while education of the masses became actively discouraged. The practitioners of the sciences became fugitives in their homeland, risking arrest and even execution should they dare share the secrets of chemistry and mechanics. And why should they have wanted to, knowing it would only be used to harm? Such gifts used in ignorance would only cause trouble.

Lena's forefathers had decided long ago to hoard the knowledge of the ancient scientists behind the protected walls of Ardmire Castle, appointing themselves guardians of what remained of a once-vast collection. It was better to live as outcasts in their own culture, they reasoned, than to let mankind's greatest achievements be lost forever. A few other families had joined them, continuing their research in obscurity and teaching their children as they had been taught, shielded by the isolation and reputation of Ardham Forest.

Lena was the last surviving member of Ardmire Castle, though she knew of others like herself across the kingdom, living in secret laboratories and fearful of one day having it all stripped from them. It was the very reason the legend of Flametongue had been born: to hide what really lay inside the castle walls.

She placed a friendly hand on the knight's arm, snatching it back with an apologetic smile when he winced in pain. She sighed. "Did you ever think the legends were just that? Stories told to keep strangers away?"

Sir Trevyr stared at her in silent disbelief. Suddenly, all the will seemed to drain from him, and he sank into a nearby chair, tears running unchecked down dirt-streaked cheeks.

"No, no, the Legend of Ardmire has to be real," he wailed. "It's our only hope. Without it, we'll never defeat Aesloras. So many people will die. My mother. My sister. Everyone I've ever known! Please tell me it's real!"

His anguished face tugged at her heart, his very real fear of losing loved ones reminding her harshly of her own father's passing. She pursed her lips tightly and shook her head, ashamed she'd ever teased him now.

"I'm sorry. It's just me here, and my books. There was never any weapon."

Sir Trevyr buried his face in his hands and openly wept, the gut-wrenching howl of a man who'd lost everything.

Politely turning away from his grief, Lena let her eyes wander over the shelves, almost wishing she did have a legendary artifact to lend him. If what he said was true, Aesloras wouldn't stop at razing the capital. The army would continue to sweep across the whole kingdom, including her isolated sanctuary. Everything her family had fought so hard to protect would be gone, left in the hands of the greedy and despotic.

Alas, all she had were her books.

Her books, filled with centuries of research, containing blueprints for contraptions, gizmos, and gadgets. Her books, with detailed instructions on how Flametongue was built and how to build more. With recipes for tars, oozes, and accelerants.

None of the inventions were weapons as the knight understood them, but with proper instruction and innovation, Lena was confident they could send the Aesloran soldiers running back to the comfort of their safe, dragon-free homes. And maybe, just maybe, the government of Kergory would be desperate enough to welcome back their ostracized kin. Perhaps, in the face of this hopeless invasion, it was time for the people to embrace the ancient teachings once more.

Sir Trevyr sniffled into his palms. "I can't believe it's all hopeless."

Lena knelt to bring her face level with his, placing a hand on his knee to draw his attention. She held the book before him as he lifted his head.

"It's not hopeless. My books! My father said the answer is always in books, and he was right!"

Sir Trevyr eyed the brandished tome skeptically. "You can use that to defeat an army?"

She shrugged with excitement. "Of course! There's more power in these books than your sword will ever wield. With just this one, we can build another Flametongue. A hundred Flametongues! No army would stand a chance. They'd probably piddle in their armor when they set eyes on a whole fleet of dragons."

The light of hope flared again in the knight's eyes, and he sat up straight in the chair. "You really think we can build a hundred machines like your dragon?"

She nodded. "It won't be easy, and I'll need the king's men to listen to my every direction, but yes. If we hurry, we can send the enemy back without risking a single life. And my family legacy will be safe."

The knight surged to his feet, knocking Lena on her rump. He reached a hand down for her, a wide smile splitting his reddened and filthy face. "Then let's leave immediately. For king and country!"

Lena accepted the hand and rose to her feet, brushing the moistness from his palm off on her skirt. "I prefer 'for peace and solitude,' but the sentiment's the same."

He grabbed her hand and tugged her toward the door. Clutching the book tightly to her chest so as not to drop it, Lena hurried along behind him. His enthusiasm was infectious, and the prospect of building a hundred machines before an enemy army could swarm over them provided just the challenge she'd been waiting for her whole life. She could single-handedly restore respect and honor to the sciences, earning the right to live openly for herself and others. This was her moment, her time to rise, and she relished every second of it.

It didn't take long to convince King Jovarn to give Lena a chance to make her dragon army a reality. The nonexistence of a magical weapon left him with little alternative. Once Sir Trevyr related his experience with the fabled Flametongue and Lena had explained how the mechanics worked, the king's curiosity even became piqued by the idea.

Lena laid out the terms of her assistance quite clearly. She would maintain control over how her inventions were used, or she and all her books would disappear forever, leaving the king and his people at the mercy of the invading force. He was more than happy to lend her control of the royal blacksmiths and resources in an effort to save his men and his rule.

As for how Lena and the sciences would fit into Kergory society after the war—well, that was a negotiation for another time and one where Lena would likely keep the upper hand.

Sir Trevyr watched as Lena patiently guided the blacksmiths in forming and bending gears, joints, lifts, and the myriad other pieces required for each automaton. He stood by her side as she divided the yeomen into teams, delegating each with a task designed to keep the flow of production effortless and brisk. He peered over her shoulder as she taught the men how to read blueprints and distributed recipes for the noxious Dragon's Breath to the kitchen staff. He learned more in the few days spent under Lena's direction than he had ever garnered over the years of study on his own.

By the time the Aesloran forces had crossed the border, a thousand men worked diligently to assemble a hundred metal defenders. And when the army crested the hill, ready to wage a quick and dirty war with the lesser forces, they found a line of clicking, hissing great wyrms shielding the capital in a wall of fire and steel.

Marching back and forth along the control panels, Lena directed the pull and twist of knobs and levers in a smooth parade of fury and intimidation. As Sir Trevyr watched from his place on the sidelines, admiration welled within him for the woman he had once thought odd and possibly insane. The way her face lit up as she shouted instructions and her command over the marvelous creations she'd fabricated was a marvel to behold.

Cheers rang from the streets as the enemy ran screaming back the way they had come. The crowd chanted Lena's name on grateful lips. This was her power, her element, and Sir Trevyr had never believed in anything more.

She was the Legend of Ardmire Castle.

All Stop

L. C. Jenkins

All Stop."

Two words—that was all it took for the world to start spinning in a completely different direction. Long after, what I remembered most was the silence that followed. A dead, still silence that gripped my soul and squeezed until I could barely breathe. Life had changed, and everyone knew it. There would be no denials, no arguments—just a grim acceptance. Life would go on as it tended to, no matter how grim or horrifying the circumstances might be, but in that moment, my own life would be different.

"All Stop."

Simone sat on the subway, her earbuds blasting songs from the eighties as she ran her eye over the ever-growing list of emails her boss sent daily. She groaned mentally, knowing her workload was becoming increasingly impossible. She'd have to have a difficult discussion soon, though whether with her boss to give him her notice or with herself to buckle down and deal, she didn't know.

She closed out her email, intent on relaxing for the next forty-five minutes.

Grateful for the privacy technology that obscured her screen from the curious eyes of strangers, Simone opened a reading app. It wasn't anything considered risqué by most of the world, but if she were caught with the fashion magazine here in Morelle, the consequences would be brutal. The little island kingdom considered such outside distractions immoral and rebellious at best and, at worst, Unproductive to the Common Cause—in other words, sedition.

Simone thought the magazine was just a bit of harmless fluff, and she loved the glimpses it provided of high couture's bright colors and creative designs. The magazine's gaudy cover and headline, *Finding Your Purpose*, had caught her eye as she quickly looked around the secret alcove of the newsstand she'd visited earlier. She hadn't hesitated to silently signal the clerk, who had flashed her a card with a QR code. Simone had handed over her bank card, and the receipt had read *Financial Update Today, Issue 42.*

In the reading app, Simone opened the copy of *Financial Update Today* and skipped to page forty-two, as directed by the coded receipt. There, set between an article about inflation and an essay on the virtues of saving, were her contraband pages of glitz and glam. Later, she would delete them, leaving her with the dull and boring world of finance.

Turning to the fashion magazine's cover article, Simone began to read.

First bullet point: *Ask yourself questions and answer truthfully.*

Simone rolled her eyes. She often questioned herself, but the last part was where she faltered.

Two: *Take chances.*

She almost laughed. The chanciest thing Simone had ever done was buy a "winter white" skirt that never saw the light of day. Her mother had never permitted her to wear white after the first of September, and she had internalized the rule. It wasn't that Simone hadn't tried to wear the skirt, but when she did, she felt like everyone would be scandalized if she left the house in it.

Three: *Learn new things. Try an adventure.*

Simone snorted. The last thing she had learned was a new cost-analysis spreadsheet, and adventures were for movies.

The last bit of advice the article gave was to "trust yourself." Simone wanted to glare at the author of the article. It was hard to trust yourself when all your decisions in life had been wrong, at least according to the society she lived in. There had been a time when she hadn't felt that way, but that had been a long time ago and she'd been very small.

The paltry article wasn't a panacea for her general dissatisfaction in life, but it gave her things to think about.

Simone sighed, closed the reading app, and settled deeper in her seat, intent on relaxing for the next half hour. She hoped the pizza shop wouldn't be too busy when she got there to pick up a few stray slices and a can of pop for dinner.

Leaning back, Simone let the eighties songs wash over her. The old songs reminded her of her mother, who would lip-sync them in the small kitchen of their apartment as she painted beautiful watercolors. She had never sung the words; she'd been embarrassed when Simone caught her just lip-syncing them. "Singing is not my talent," she had said. Simone hadn't disagreed, but her mother's voice had always been beautiful to her, so Simone had encouraged her mother to sing anyway. Her mother had rarely obliged, but at least she'd continued enjoying music in her small way.

The old Bon Jovi song "Runaway" finished, and "Cruel Summer" by Bananarama came on. Simone only remembered the name of the group because it was such a funny name.

"The eighties were like that," her mother had told her. "Happy, bright, and fairly carefree. Very few things were serious or doom and gloom. The whole world seemed to be optimistic."

Simone was a bit jealous of that idyllic time. Her whole life, the world had seemed a complete wreck: Wars, climate change, politics, women's rights, racial inequality, drug abuse. It all seemed out of control. The eighties—well, she could definitely understand the fascination and her mother's reluctance to leave such a time for the acid pit it was now.

Simone wondered what the music of her generation would have sounded like if they'd been allowed to create any.

The refrain had just started for the second time when the music suddenly stopped. After a small beat of time, an emergency signal bleated over her earphones, and Simone hurried to turn down the volume. But instead of the comforting words that usually began, "This is a test," the emergency signal was followed by the words, "All Stop."

In utter shock, Simone pulled the earbuds from her ears and looked around. Surely this was some kind of malfunction. The other commuters were doing the same, looking at each other in slowly dawning horror.

A woman in the back whispered, "Did you just hear . . . ?"

"The call for an All Stop?" a man finished for her.

Slowly, hesitantly, one voice and then another murmured agreement.

"Surely it isn't real, right?" a young man asked.

Simone looked at him. He was most likely a college student, judging by his attire, but suddenly he looked like a nine-year-old, lost and alone.

"Do you have somewhere to go?" she asked.

He nodded, but she could see he was starting to panic. Truthfully, they all probably were. Her own palms were clammy, her breathing a bit shallower than it should be, and her heart was pounding. There was comfort in knowing she wasn't the only one on edge and apprehensive. Sure, there had been drills for this, and they were hopefully all prepared for it; that was the law, anyway. But drills weren't reality.

"Attention, all passengers. An All Stop has been called. We have verified it is legitimate. There is no need to exit before your planned stop. We will be continuing our routes for the next twenty-four hours. You will be able to get to your designated safe place." The conductor paused. In a shaky voice, he added, "God bless us all."

A few hushed amens echoed around Simone, and one or two people even crossed themselves. She glanced quickly at the electronic board at the front of the car: *Zone 2.* Her breath caught. She was still four zones from home. She could do nothing but wait and worry.

The whole train remained eerily silent as they listened for the cause of the alarm, but nothing could be heard over the monotonous sound of the train smoothly sliding along the rails. There were no impatient taps of a toe, no one keeping the beat of a song on their thigh, no muffled crying. Just that horrible silence. The one that enveloped a person as they faced down their mounting fear, ran contingency plans in their head, reviewed what they were supposed to be doing, and considered how the situation would affect their life, family, and friends.

As they neared Zone Three, the silence grated on Simone's nerves. It became louder than any noise she had ever experienced. It almost seemed like a spell, and to break it would also break the tenuous seam of the old world she and the other passengers clung to.

As the conductor's voice came back on the PA system minutes from Station Three, the relief in the car was palpable.

"Ladies and gentlemen, at the next stop, ushers and attendants will be available to help you with travel arrangements should you need help getting to your safe location. Our train will be delayed thirty minutes so those with questions can be helped. Do not exit the train unless you need assistance."

The message was soothing, despite the extraordinary words. A train conductor making an announcement was something they knew. It happened all the time. It was normal, assuming you could ignore the words.

Simone couldn't. The words annoyed her. She knew it was necessary; not everyone would be near their designated area. Some people would have been on business trips or shopping trips in the city; others would immediately need to leave for the airports. But for those who knew where they were going, the added delay just increased their barely contained panic.

If only we knew why the All Stop had been called.

Mentally running down the list of possibilities for such an emergency wasn't helping her panic. The options were catastrophic and horrifying. She wasn't sure if she should be grateful she was stuck underground, where she couldn't see what might be going on, or if she should rue her bad luck, which left her imagining worst-case scenarios in the absence of facts.

Simone wished she could call her family: her mother, her sister, Celeste, anyone. But her phone, along with everyone else's, would be a useless brick for who knew how long. The signals would have been commandeered for emergency services. Most people's single job right now was to get to their safe spot as quickly and efficiently as possible, with no distractions to slow them down or prevent them from following directions from public officials.

With that in mind, Simone packed away her earphones and other belongings to help make room on the train car. Others would be joining them, and in an All Stop, it was one seat per passenger. There would be no quarreling over seats; those already aboard were to slide over and leave aisle seats for newcomers.

Upon their arrival at Station Three, an usher entered the car. "Attention! We will be seating cars by zones. At your stop, you will exit the car to the left." He began to call out zones, assigning each person a seat and giving them an exit number. Simone was the second person seated in Zone Six, so she would be the second to last to leave the car.

The car was full when it finally sped off down the track; the Zone Six section had swelled to thirty people. Simone cursed herself for living in such a popular neighborhood, but it was where she had always lived, and until this moment, she had never wanted to move.

By the time they reached Zone Five, the car consisted almost entirely of Zone Six passengers. It would take fifteen to twenty minutes for them all to disembark. How long had they been on the train since the All Stop began? What time was it?

Simone asked the usher, who glanced down at his old-fashioned watch. She used to think it funny that they still wore them, but now she wished she had her own. "It's seven p.m., miss."

Simone's legs were shaky when she finally stood to leave. Would they be urged to stay at the station? There had been drills for that, but there had also been drills for leaving the station and going home.

She wasn't sure which answer she'd prefer.

Simone found her designated exit by muscle memory rather than thought. Another uniformed usher stood at the bottom of the stairs, a single-file line in front of him. At his side stood two emergency workers, one in an Order uniform and the other in a Heal uniform, while farther down, at another set of stairs, stood emergency workers in a Fire uniform and a Peace uniform. Simone had hoped one would be missing; that would have provided a clue about the emergency.

The line moved quickly as, one by one, they were released to go upstairs. When it was her turn, the usher only asked for her address.

"Take car number four. Let the driver know you're the last passenger for this trip."

She climbed into the dark car, a large touring model that felt small with so many passengers, and five minutes later, the driver let her out on her own block. Simone had turned to walk home when a hand touched her shoulder, and she jumped in surprise.

It was Alex, the owner of the pizza shop. "Sorry," he muttered, looking around quickly. He shoved a bag into her hand. "It's your usual Tuesday order. I probably won't be selling any for a while, so I wanted to make sure you had my last one. I know we haven't gotten to talk a lot about our friendship, but I'd planned to ask you out when you came in tonight."

Simone smiled sadly. "I would have said yes." It hadn't been her love of pizza that kept her coming in every Tuesday. It had been Alex and the snippets of conversations they had over all the little things. Just the ability to share their days had been a blessing.

He leaned over and kissed her gently on the cheek. "Well, when this is over, maybe we can actually have that date." He smiled widely. "Now off you go before I'm seen out here."

Simone nodded quickly but left him with a kiss on his own cheek. It was very unlike her; normally, she was shy and reserved. However, there was too much unknown right now to hold back. If disaster was looming, she wanted him to know she cared.

She walked swiftly down the block. She could see no obvious signs of distress. She started to hope it was an elaborate drill or a malfunction of the system.

That is, until a shadow fell over her, and the loud *shoop* of a helicopter sounded overhead. The noise was immense in the quiet, echoing like a thunderclap between the close buildings. Simone looked up but saw nothing. A chill ran down her back as her palms began to sweat, and she resisted the urge to run for her front door. Running in an All Stop was against the law. Everything had to be orderly and calm; lives depended on it.

Twenty feet from her door, the shadow loomed again, but Simone didn't dare look up, too afraid it wasn't the helicopter she had assumed. She trained her eyes on an older man ahead of her, walking toward her. She timed her breathing with his slow, even footsteps. One, in; two, out. One, in; two, out. One—

She stopped dead in her tracks. He was gone! She glanced around. There were a few other people, but no one else seemed to have noticed the man's disappearance. There was no doorway he could have ducked into, as far as she knew. Could she have imagined him? She didn't think so.

Then Simone saw a little, dark car parked in a nearby alley and hastily averted her gaze. She recognized it as belonging to the King's Guard. Trembling, she walked as quickly as she dared to her front stoop.

Ten minutes later, she was in her apartment, rushing to replace her flimsy work attire and heels with jeans, T-shirt, and tennis shoes. She pulled out her prepacked bag, which included a few changes of clothes, toiletries, emergency provisions, and her ID and travel docu-ments, in case the call came to evacuate. She dropped it by the front door.

Sitting on the sofa, she opened the takeout bag Alex had given her and ate as slowly as she dared. The TV was on, but all it displayed was *Standby for further instructions.*

Thirty minutes passed, and still there was no word. She tried the radio, but nothing was forthcoming. She began to watch out the win-dow, becoming increasingly anxious as the world grew dark around her.

Lights flipped on. She wished she weren't alone; that was the hardest part. She could see some of her neighbors huddling around TVs as silent as hers, but they were at least together.

She thought about Alex, who lived alone above the pizza shop.

Should she risk it? There would be a fine if the authorities caught her somewhere she wasn't registered to be during an All Stop. A huge fine and jail time. Some had even been put to death. The rules were in place to ensure everyone's safety, that everyone had a way out. The plans had been drawn up specifically with that in mind. That was why the train hadn't been overwhelmed, why there had been an empty seat for Simone in the car from the station. It had been reserved for her. If Alex were in a different group, her presence would throw the plans off. It could lead to her death or the death of some other innocent person.

The old maps!

There were perks to having a father who'd been a cartographer. The maps would tell her which evacuation route Alex lived on. If it were the same as hers, it wouldn't be such a risk.

She ran to her mother's old room and rummaged through the desk where her mother had kept the maps. They were sacred to her because Simone's father had been part of the team that had drawn them up. After his death, anything he had touched had been preserved, including his master index of maps. All the maps he'd ever drawn were in that book, and he'd wanted to map everything.

Simone found her zone and then her evacuation group. Alex's building was in the same group! There was even a subway access tunnel running along her street toward Alex's building that the basement of her building had access to.

She rejoiced in her good luck, but her joy was short-lived. What would Alex think if she showed up at his place? Would he be appalled? Even if she could make it there with her fully packed bag, food could become an issue. Alex would be provisioned for one, just as she was; neither could sustain the other for an extended period.

Simone wouldn't go. She always did the right thing, the expected thing. She followed the rules and helped others when she could. It had never failed her, so why change?

Just then, the TV sprang to life.

"Attention, all residents of Morelle and the surrounding areas. It has been determined that the best course of action is to shelter in place.

Do not leave your safe places. If you need assistance, call the appropriate service, and you will be taken care of accordingly. This order will be in place until further notice. The All Stop was declared by the court after a series of odd occurrences around the palace. We have little information to disseminate at this time. We value your cooperation and patience and will update you as we learn more."

It was odd that the All Stop had been declared only by the court and not in conjunction with the palace. However, General Alverton, the country's leader in all but name, had died just two weeks ago. Things were bound to be a bit out of order.

Simone was more concerned with the order to shelter in place. She'd never liked that option, nor had her mother. It was one reason her mother had moved out of the city; she needed room to roam, and Celeste's place had acres.

Simone sighed and searched for her cell phone. It was still useless. It was approaching her normal bedtime, but it didn't matter; there would be no sleep for her tonight. Again, she longed for Alex. If he were here, they could sleep in shifts, waiting for information.

Despite her anxiety, she fell asleep on the sofa, fully dressed.

When Simone woke, the apartment was dark. She must have gotten at least two hours of sleep as the TV was now off. Fumbling in the dark, she found the remote and hit the button to turn the TV back on.

It remained dark.

Simone frowned and sat up, realizing, too, that the lights had been on when she'd laid down to read. Did the electricity go out? She glanced out the windows to see that no one had light. That was ominous. The power grid should have been secure. Unless there was a natural disaster, but there'd been no evidence of that when she'd walked home.

Simone got up to find her emergency lights, which she'd put in the dining alcove. She found the little battery-operated light and hit the small switch. As the light bloomed in the dark room, she heard a very faint, shrill whistle, which died into a low grumble. The sky outside lit up for just a second.

Simone walked fearfully to the window. She knew that sound. The same sound had accompanied the death of her father so many years before.

Her eyes went to a water glass sitting on the table; the water shook ever so slightly. Watching the glass, she was ten again.

Simone's father had been anxious and grumpy leading up to that night, and that evening was no different. He came home, walked straight to the kitchen, and filled a glass with water. He placed it on the table and bid Simone and Celeste to watch the water.

At first, they thought it was some kind of magic trick, but her father left the room to talk to her mother. As hushed, fevered voices drifted from the other room, Celeste went back to playing with her doll. Simone stayed at the table, but she lost focus, too engrossed in her sketch pad.

It wasn't until water splattered her drawing that she looked up again. The glass was no longer still; water sloshed over its rim. By then, Simone could feel the rumble under her feet.

"Dad!" she called, softly at first and then louder as she realized her parents weren't paying attention. "Dad!"

He ran to the table and swore. It was the first and last time she ever heard her father swear. "They're coming this way, Vivienne. We have to leave now."

Her mother grabbed Celeste and handed each girl a coat and a small backpack. Celeste clung to her doll, while Simone snatched her sketchbook and colored pencils, cramming them into the backpack.

Turning out the lights, her father went to the window. "Who's coming?" Simone asked, not really expecting an answer. Her father knelt beside her and pointed out the window.

That's when she saw the tank. Simone had seen tanks before, on the parade grounds around the palace or on parade during holiday, but it looked very out of place on their residential street.

"The soldiers," her father whispered.

Simone was confused. The soldiers were there for their protection; everyone knew that. But her father seemed very afraid.

"It's too late, Vi."

Her mother paled. "What do we do?"

Her father only shook his head helplessly. "We can only hope—" His voice faltered, and he looked meaningfully at Simone and her sister before he became brisk and businesslike. "Hide those bags and take off your coats and shoes."

He pulled up the carpet and pried up several floorboards. There was a treasure trove of objects already there: several books that had disappeared from the family bookshelves weeks before and rolled-up canvases, an easel, and paints from her mother's studio.

"Simone, I want your sketch pad and pencils."

She handed them to her father, wide-eyed, too shocked to protest. He threw them in and replaced the boards, while her mother stood at the window, reciting numbers—numbers Simone now realized, looking out the same window, corresponded to the neighboring buildings.

Her father then handed Simone a calculator and an old ledger her mother had used to keep track of sales. "You want to grow up to be an accountant. Remember that. Not a singer and not an artist."

Then he turned to Celeste and asked what she wanted to be when she grew up. She beamed. "A mommy."

He smiled. "Good girl."

Her mother turned from the window. "Lewis . . ."

He nodded, and his eyes momentarily filled with tears. "They don't know who you are, Vi. It's going to be fine."

Except it wouldn't be fine.

Her father had urged them back to their usual evening activities just minutes before the soldiers knocked on the door with such force, the plaster surrounding it cracked. Their mother hurried over to answer the door. The first soldier's eyes met Simone's and then Celeste's before he turned to his fellows. He gave a quick hand signal for them to remain in the hall.

Simone's mother tried to be polite. "Yes, can I help you?"

"We're looking for Lewis Windmere, the cartographer. Our records indicate he lives here."

"I'll go get him."

As she walked out of the room, the soldier turned to Simone. "What are you studying?"

"Ar—" The soldier's eyebrows raised. "Accounting," Simone corrected quickly. He nodded, satisfied.

"I want to be a mommy," Celeste chimed in. The soldier smiled and patted her hair.

Simone's father walked out of the kitchen with a coffee cup. "I'm Windmere." He set the cup down on the table, next to the glass.

The soldier nodded once and turned to Simone's mother. "Ma'am, if you could take the children into the next room, we'd like to question your husband."

They sat in the bedroom for what seemed like hours, her mother peeping through the door. Her father's voice, quiet but firm, drifted reassuringly back to them.

"But it isn't art; it's a science," he argued, finally getting loud. But Lewis Windmere's maps had always been ornate and highly decorated. There was no denying they elevated the hard facts of mapmaking to an art form.

In the end, it didn't matter. Moments later, there was a loud bang. Her mother screamed and tried to run for the living room, only to be held back by a soldier standing at the end of the hallway. They never said a word to the hysterical woman or the two wide-eyed, crying children. Simone never saw her father's body, just the bloodstain on the rug.

They left the apartment the next day; the army allowed them to leave the city for Simone's grandparents' house in the country. It was more than a month before they returned. The rug had been replaced and the plaster fixed, but the glass had remained on the table next to her father's coffee cup.

As a child, Simone had seen the events as a mystery, but as an adult, she knew what had happened. A small segment of disgruntled military personnel who believed the king was too heavily influenced by outsiders had attempted a coup. Hundreds of creative people had been killed in the capital alone, and there had been outright war for three weeks. The king became a puppet, but life went on. Simone's mother got a regular job, while Simone and her sister grew up to become just what they'd told the soldiers.

And now the tanks were outside again. There'd been speculation for days, but Simone had simply dismissed all the whispering as wishful thinking. The king had announced the general's death himself, but there had been no mention of his "contributions to society," his career, or even his actual service. Just a bare-bones declaration and then silence.

The rumbling stopped, and she glanced out the window. There at the corner was a tank, just like so many years before. In fact, it could have been the same one. The only question was whom it belonged to: the king trying to take back his country or simply another faction trying to gain power?

A second question followed at its heels: what did it mean for her? She had done what she was supposed to, and she wasn't any safer now than she had been as a child.

Hurried footsteps sounded in the hall. Simone whirled around to face the door. As she did, her foot caught, and she fell.

The footsteps receded, and Simone took a deep, calming breath. She glanced at her feet, which were now tangled in the rug, and spied what she had caught her foot on: a loose floorboard.

She bent to fix it, trying to ignore the ugly stained wood, when she spied a red pencil. Hesitantly, she reached underneath the floor and pulled out her old sketch pad and pencils. The cover had been light gray, but a horrible, vicious brown covered most of it now.

Her father's blood.

Simone's hand trembled as she opened the stuck pages to a fourth of the way in. There, she found where she'd left off that night. She'd been drawing a dragon, one of the two creatures that held up the crest of the kingdom. He was only half finished—a metaphor for her own half-finished life, she realized, suddenly blinded by tears. She began to sob, not only for her father but for the little girl whose life had been so irretrievably altered.

The rumbling started up again outside, but it barely registered in Simone's grief. Her father had given his life for art. He'd had no chance to hide his gifts; he'd been well known and successful. Her mother had been a highly successful painter, but she had always hidden her identity because she never wanted to be famous. She had just wanted to paint in peace. Simone's father had given his life so her mother might have a chance to paint again one day or sing with abandon. He had given his life so Simone and her sister might one day have a life in which they weren't accountants or moms unless they wanted to be. He'd given his life for that cause because he'd believed in it. Believed in them.

Simone dried her tears.

The tank on the street meant her life was about to change again. She didn't know if the tank was friend or foe. What she did know was she wasn't a little girl anymore. She could choose, and like her father, she could make a stand.

The silly article she'd read earlier came back to her; it was silly and superficial, but she had nothing else. Her old life with her father was too distant for her to glean anything from it, and the life she'd been living since his death was a lie. She was alone in this moment, and that silly article was all she had.

"Ask yourself questions and answer truthfully."

Was she ready to die for her art, like her father had? Did she believe she could change the world?

The answers weren't easy yeses or noes as she'd hoped. The world was too nuanced and complex. She wasn't sure she was prepared to die for anything, but she didn't want to live as an accountant. As for changing the world, Simone wasn't really worried about the whole world or even her little country. She did believe she could change her own path, though.

"Take chances."

Simone pulled one of her mother's watercolor paintings out from under the floorboards. Pulling down an old frame, she replaced the boring, mass-produced landscape within with her mother's ethereal, whimsical scene of flowers and fairies and put it back on the wall where it belonged.

"Learn new things."

Simone looked at her childish drawing of a dragon. It was good, but it would get better, she vowed. Learning to draw might take time, but for now . . .

"Try an adventure" sounded better. She walked back to her father's map index, smiling as she placed it and the old drawing pad and pencils into her bag by the door. She hefted the bag up to her shoulder. She would see whether Alex was up for an adventure. If so, that would be great, but if not, that would be fine too.

"Trust yourself."

Simone thought about that for a moment. She wasn't sure she was making the right decision—wasn't sure she could trust herself all at once—but she could trust herself in this moment. And maybe one day, after enough moments of trusting herself, she would become the person she truly wanted to be.

Conversion

Ynes Malakova

ome on, come on.

Delilah pressed the heel of her hand against the flimsy white slab that was her desk.

For now.

After three soulless years, she was due a promotion.

When she had first started her job at the agency, she was fresh-faced and naive, carrying a tender enthusiasm on her shoulders. Her eyes and her smile had sparkled in the halls, and she had rolled her insights out like blankets, unpacking baskets of fresh ideas in front of her coworkers. Ideas they had snatched up and devoured, until she was fleshless and ragged, shattered and tossed about like a bleached bone tumbling in the waves, scraping the workroom floor with each rise and fall of the tide.

Time flies.

She fanned her fingers wide. Under the fluorescent light, they resembled birch trees: smooth, elongated trunks spattered with flaws—circles—stretched wide like mouths agape with surprise or woven in tight clusters, jigsawing across her joints.

Hives were terrible.

She clicked her mouse over the refresh button. Still nothing.

Three o'clock sharp. That's what they said.

She drummed her fingers on her desk, stretching her knuckles to alleviate the swelling in the thick pad of skin where fingers met palm.

Click. Still nothing.

She had thought she was past the point of hives; it was such a rookie problem. She had leaped far beyond stress, floated far above pain. She scoffed and rolled her eyes, repeating the word that had saved her, the word she had coveted after months of sweeping up shards of her splintered heart from the workroom floor. The word that had become her mantra.

Conversion.

The printer moaned, spewing an endless array of numbers and charts.

Delilah shifted her focus to her second monitor. She clawed apart emails while she sipped her tea, blowing at her cup and pushing the steam toward the monitor. She enjoyed burning through messages, melting all the silly, irrelevant words until all that remained was the white-hot, smoldering heart of the sale.

She treasured that heart. She needed it.

Delilah tapped impatiently on her mouse again. Nothing. *Nothing!* She leaned back in her chair and peeked out of her cubicle, her gaze falling on the back of her friend Chandry's head.

Chandry had started at the agency only a year ago. She was a creature of habit. Each day, she parted her hair in the same place, dressed in bright blouses decorated with perfectly aligned geometric patterns, and brought the same brand of yogurt for breakfast—which she ate at exactly 8:05 a.m.

While Delilah's flame incinerated all frivolous noise, Chandry's flame made tiny, meticulous cuts. Their flames twined together and danced with a movement both fluid and controlled, flashing like a kaleidoscope of wings taking to the skies.

To the agency, it had looked like a surge of clicks and conversions in quarter one. Sales had tripled, and they had been projected to break records when quarter two closed.

At first, Delilah and Chandry had had working lunches in the agency's small kitchen—but their success took them beyond the stark white walls, into trendy sandwich joints and make-your-own salad buffets. In these spaces, their conversations had shifted from sales and slides to colors and dreams. Sipping a bright-orange ginger-and-carrot smoothie, Chandry had spoken of her love of monarchs, her dream, one day, of having a garden to help them feed and thrive. Delilah had shared her passion for dancing, a dying dream she had given up when her partner asked to start a family together.

Midway through quarter three, the agency proudly announced their growth had opened new doors: a search for a supervisor would begin. While they would be exploring all angles, they encouraged employees with creativity and ambition from their Marketing and Sales division to apply.

When Delilah and Chandry slept, they dreamed of conversions.

Delilah reached for a stack of flat-colored folders on her desk that housed hundreds of metrics: insights from days spent running focus groups and evenings spent chained to her desk under an artificial light, lurking in reports, collecting metrics, counting them all up like coins.

No matter how she looked at it, sales were beginning to decline.

Delilah lifted the top folder from her stack and prepared to walk it to the CEO's desk. She could get the jump on the problem, prove her quick wit and perception while leaving Chandry in the dark.

By all means, she should have.

Delilah glanced ruefully at the photograph on her desk. A newborn baby girl with puckered lips stared back at her with bright blue eyes.

Sales were not the only thing that had grown exponentially in the first two quarters of the year.

She had grown a life inside her.

Delilah peered down at the folder, stacked with problems. Something within her stirred, and her heart fluttered with guilt.

She walked to Chandry's cubicle and laid the folder neatly on her desk.

We'll figure it out together.

At 3:17 p.m., Delilah's computer chimed. Her heart jerked, plugging her throat momentarily, and her gaze darted to her screen.

Subject: Promotion.

She clicked it open with a swollen, shaky finger.

We are excited to promote Chandry Evans to Marketing and Sales supervisor. Her dedication, quick analysis, and action have kept us on a strong upward trend.

Reporting to Chandry will be Mike Owens, Delilah Francis.

Delilah buried her face in her hands. Her fingers burned, then quivered, then burned. Throughout her life, Delilah had met many dragons: the kindergarten teacher who roared at children, the professor with the sharp pen that made essays bleed, and even the occasional acquaintance who preferred the taste of ridicule over flesh, sinking his teeth into competencies like a thick femur bone. But of all the dragons Delilah had ever encountered, Chandry was perhaps the most cunning.

A patterned sleeve peeked past the wall of Delilah's cubicle. Beneath it hung a tightly pressed ream of charts and graphs.

"Good morning."

Delilah rolled her eyes. It wasn't a good morning. There were no more good mornings.

"What do you need from me?" The question had broken Delilah for weeks.

Chandry spread her papers across Delilah's desk. Delilah wondered just how long Mike had spent under fire, preparing those graphs. "Sales are down this month. I need you to tell me why."

Delilah looked at the chaotic stacks of paper piled in every direction on her desk. She combed her fingers across her lap, studying her wrinkled trousers.

Gee. I wonder why.

"Hey. Del. Snap out of it." Chandry snapped her fingers to emphasize her words. "I need a full report on the conversions by six tonight. Make sure it includes an updated analysis for our new launch."

Delilah's gaze shifted to the framed picture of her daughter.

A fire formed in her gut, and she furled her fingers into a fist. Her fire bellowed as it grew, forked flames licking the bottom of her heart, and pelts of pain flickered against her ribs. Delilah shifted her focus, locking gazes with Chandry. Her eyes narrowed in defiance, her lip and cheek twitching with fury. She drew in a breath and pressed her tongue to her palate, preparing to breathe fire.

Her lips parted in anticipation, but her gaze flicked back to her daughter's face. Delilah's fire caught in her throat, and she wheezed.

I gave up my heart.

But it grew back inside me.

She thought back to the aches of pregnancy: sore, swollen feet, aching back, bouts of nausea. Her longing to dance.

Some aches simply never went away.

"Do you understand the expectation?" Chandry's voice cut through Delilah's thoughts like a scalpel.

Delilah nodded feebly, choking on her pain.

"Better get cracking," Chandry chided. She tapped a graph with a polished fingernail. "And just so you know, your ass is on the line."

Delilah sighed. She took a deep breath. "Do you remember how we used to be friends?"

Chandry's papers hit Delilah's desk with a clack. "Don't start with me, Del. I did what I had to do. It's good work, and I've gotta pay the bills."

"I've got a daughter, Chandry."

The women locked gazes in silence. Finally, Chandry rubbed her eyes. "There were never going to be two winners in this game, Del."

Delilah's arm shot forward, and she took Chandry's hand in hers. "It isn't too late for us. We could get out of here, you know. You and me. We could chase our dreams, do things our way." She lowered her voice to a whisper. "The two of us—we'd be unstoppable."

"A dancer and a gardener?" Chandry scoffed. "Don't be ridiculous. You will learn this when you're older." She tucked her papers under her arm. "If you want to survive, there are parts of yourself you have to sacrifice. You cut ties and compartmentalize."

"You mean you give up your heart."

Chandry shrugged. "Don't be so dramatic. I need your conversion report by six today."

Delilah scrawled in the margins of her notepad, looked at her writing, and scribbled over her notes. It just didn't make sense—none of it. The numbers were there, but she could not bring herself to look at them anymore.

She rolled her neck from side to side and caught a ray of sunshine spilling through her blinds. She pulled the cord, and her cubicle blazed with light.

Fresh air. That's what she needed. She had been cooped up for far too long. She picked up her notepad and folders and moved quickly down the corridor, taking the long path to avoid Chandry's brand-new office. She pressed her palm against the agency's front door and stepped outside, allowing the sun to warm the top of her head.

Delilah smiled—a wide, toothy grin that pushed at her cheeks. The breeze played with her hair, and she tilted her head back and let the sunshine warm her nose.

She heard a sudden slap at her feet and turned sharply in its direction. The pages of her notepad fluttered against the gravel like wings. Delilah watched page after page of numbers and percentages turn over.

Delilah stretched her arms wide and surrendered her folders to the parking lot—crisp, white leaves scattering across the pavement, leaping past curbs and dancing around tires until they disappeared from view.

Behind her, Delilah heard Chandry call her name, but she paid it no mind.

She had found the conversion that mattered above all others.
Time to fly.

About the Authors

In a previous life, C. D. Lombardi was a certified computer geek and project manager. Now, he writes speculative fiction and believes magic is just advanced technology we do not yet understand. When not writing, C. D. enjoys photography, woodworking, and crafts ranging from artwork such as painting and 3D printing to making furniture.

C. D. enjoys coffee. So much so, he not only grinds but also roasts his coffee beans. Rumor has it, C. D. stands for "coffee delizioso." Some of his favorite beans include Timor Organic Maubesse FTO, Monsoon Malabar, and Colombian Supremo.

Chaz Beebe lives in the world of the imaginary. Newly minted as a published author, Chaz has haunted the halls of schools, in person and online, for more than a decade. Driven to help build resiliency, knowledge, and passion for life in those in need, he aims to create a world of belonging, hope, and support through his words and deeds.

His work can be found in *Fractured Realities* and *Shadows Redefined* and now has the honor of being in *Dragons Within: Embracing Her Fire*.

You can follow Chaz on Facebook at @ChazBeebeAuthor. He is also part of the Adorkably Eclectic artistic team, which you can support at www.patreon.com/AdorkablyEclectic.

D.B. Smyth is a Molotov cocktail in Hello Kitty packaging who believes imaginary characters and make-believe worlds offer greater insight into the human condition than history books full of facts. She's on a mission to break toxic cultural norms and help multicolored sheep like her feel seen through stories that shine a light in dark spaces. D.B. writes of monsters, trauma, and the gritty parts of life in hopes we might find redemption in the darkness and beauty in the chaos. You can find her clicking away on her keyboard near Salt Lake City, Utah.

To read more from D.B. Smyth, or just to say hi, stop by @db_smyth on Instagram.

Jaumarro "Joy" Cuffee is a never-say-die writer who enjoys murder and mystery, cooking and baking, singing and . . . not broiling to death in the Texas sun. She detests the macabre but delights in "whodunits" and "howcatchems." Her lasagna is a killer, and her cakes are literally to die for—or at least worth fighting for a slice.

After decades of writing information technology copy, Joy is turning her hand to killing a few people—on the page, of course. With murder on her mind, she met with myriad magical authors in Word Splurge and dreamed up her first fantasy as an offering for *Dragons Within: Embracing Her Fire.*

Joy continues the quest to embrace her fire with murderous stories, poetry, and whatever sparks her imagination along the way. Join Joy as she unravels the mystery of writing and continues her never-ending story at @FindingMyJoy on Facebook and jaumarro.net.

When not being trained in medieval sword fighting, JoAnne Turner writes stories about queer, neurodivergent girls with weapons who play with dragons. She has been awarded for her fantasy flash fiction by the Writers Guild of Texas, where she currently serves as a board member. In her spare time, she researches dragon anatomy and dyslexic type-setters, knits dragon-scale gauntlets, and fosters an abundance of playful kittens. She lives in Dallas, Texas, with her husband and four cats. Kitten pictures and other works can be found on Instagram and Twitter at @TokenGeekGirl and her website, TokenGeekGirl.blog.

K. A. Moore is a writer, poet, con-noisseur of fantasy worlds, full-time mom, and kick-ass wife. She has loved the written word since the first time she picked up a book. Her stories illuminate brave, resilient characters who rise above their traumas and difficulties to conquer the world. A lover of all things coffee, chocolate, books, and musical theater, you can usually find her nose-deep in a book or arguing with her characters. When she's not playing referee to her four children, she binge-watches way too much *Outlander* and *Bridgerton* in her Southeast Missouri home. You can catch a glimpse of her many shenanigans at @k.a.mooreauthor on Instagram or on her Facebook author page, @KAMooreAuthor.

L. C. Jenkins has always had a love of books and reading. She has not always had a love of writing. "It's hard." Unable to find the types of stories she wanted to read, she began writing down her daydreams. Since then, she has happily found many new books to read, but she continues to document the lives of the imaginary people in her head.

L. C. lives in Northeast Ohio with her husband and adult progeny, of which there are two. When she isn't staring off into space, communing with her inner muse, she's playing with yarn, decorating rooms, or watching YouTube videos. You can visit her at TheMeanderingCamel.com.

Lex Night was born and raised in California. They have a deep fascination for cults and serial killers, to the point where friends have deemed them the "potential serial killer" of the group. They are queer, pagan, and a numerology aficionado.

A champion of quick comebacks and spot-on analogies, they write with passion and a reminder to always be the magic you want to see in the world. You can find several stories by them in the anthology *Shadows Redefined.* You can follow them on Facebook and Twitter at @LexTheAuthor for the latest information on upcoming releases.

Nikolai Wisekal's love for storytelling began with his wonderful aunt, whose stories made him laugh, think, and read everything he could get his hands on. His mother had wonderful editions of the original Grimm's fairy tales, which he enjoyed as a child. Eventually, he began to read series like the Dragonriders of Pern, Lord of the Rings, the Foundation Trilogy, and the Dresden Files, which set him on the path of fantasy and sci-fi fan for life.

He got the wibbly-wobbly idea that he could learn to write at the age of sixteen, beginning a ten-year start/stop pattern as a writer. After attending DFWCon 2018 and making friends, he started to dig into everything writing entails: characters, structure, dialogue, and his long-hated enemy, grammar. If you ask his critique partners, he has a personal vendetta against commas.

Rachael Denessen loves to explore between shadows. Drawn to both darkness and light, she reveals worlds normally blurred to our eyes. She stalks the curious creatures who dwell within them and faithfully depicts the chaos that occurs when these shadows collide. She believes it's the most fantastical and impossible stories that hold our deepest truths.

Her stories are all about connection: how characters connect with one another, themselves, and you. What values do we share? What can we learn from one another? What comfort can we find in that?

In the real world, Rachael can be found on Maui with her son, husband, and demon cat, Azazel. On the internet, she can be found surrounding herself with words on Facebook and Instagram at @rachaeldenessen and on TikTok at @rachaeldenessenauthor.

Fantasy author Sianyn Leigh grew up reading old fairy tales at her grandmother's knee, which instilled in her a passion for history, mythology, and the importance of storytelling. Obsessed with the rich pantheons, folklore, and superstitions of the world, she enjoys exploring the "what ifs" of life and weaving them into fanciful tales. Infinitely more entertained by rich fantasy than reality, Sianyn shares her musings with the world in hopes others may also be entertained.

When not writing, Sianyn can be found binge-watching her favorite TV shows, taking on home-improvement projects, and hosting her local writing group. You can read a sampling of her short stories and find links to her work at www.sianynleigh.com.

Ynes Malakova is the black sheep in a family of wolves. Beauty in darkness is her magic, her love, and her moon. A fan of the pastel-goth aesthetic, she collects adorably sinister plushies and pleasantly disturbing scented candles. She has authored several award-winning and bestselling short stories, which can be found on her bookshelf above her mini Zen graveyard.

Want to win her heart? Buy her a dozen white roses, recite a William Blake poem—or just cook dinner and put on a slasher film. She enjoys conversations about artwork, literature published before 1800, and the connections between innocence, femininity, serpents, and death. On weekends, she breaks out board games with friends, particularly Mansions of Madness, which she plays exclusively as William Yorick.

Come say hi on social media at @ynesmalakova. She probably won't bite.

9 781947 012097